DAMON

DAY & KNIGHT SERIES BOOK 1

AUBREE VALENTINE

Damon
Copyright © 2020 by Aubree Valentine
All rights reserved.
All rights reserved worldwide.

No part of this book may be reproduced, copied or transmitted in any medium, whether electronic, internet or otherwise, without the expressed permission of the author. This is a work of fiction. All characters, events, locations, and names occurring in this book are the product of the author's imagination or are the property of their respective owners and are used fictitiously. Any resemblances to actual events, locations, or persons (living or dead), is entirely coincidental and not intended by the author. All trademarks and trade names are used in a fictitious manner and are in no way endorsed by or an endorsement of their respective owners.
May contain sexual situations, violence, sensitive and offensive language, and mature topics.
Recommended for age 18 years and up.

Cover Image: Shelley Lange Photography featuring
Model: Kris Zizzo
Cover Design: Mignon Mykel with Oh So Novel

ONE
DAMON

Growing up thirty miles outside of Hershey, PA, in a little farming town by the name of Bitterhill with a population of less than a thousand people means that everyone knows everyone. The entire town shuts down for Friday night football, weddings, and funerals. Our school system still consists of just one building for preschool all the way up until freshman year of high school, when we all go to the county high school until graduation.

Nearly every boy that stayed in this town has married a girl he's known since he was born. It may sound awful, but there's also a good chance that we've all dated one of our buddy's girls at one time too. Only the ones who got the hell out of here end up marrying someone new.

Gavin and Quinn? They fall into the first scenario. Gavin and Quinn have been in love with each other since middle school, and I think we all knew that one day we'd be standing here watching the two of them exchange vows.

The entire town is seated in our little small-town church. Not a single store or business is open today. Each pew is full of familiar faces that I've known my entire life. Pastor Harold, who has been the minister at this church for as long as I can remember, is officiating the ceremony while Gavin and Quinn's parents look on from the front row with pride.

As his best man, I've got the distinct honor of being at his side. My twin brother Curtis and another of our childhood friends – Stone Montgomery – serve as the groomsmen.

Back in the day, the four of us were inseparable until high school, where shit got weird, and Stone seemed to fall out of touch with everyone. Then shortly after graduation, me and my brother joined the military and got the hell out of town for a while.

Unlike Curtis, I came back after a four-year stint in the Navy and took over the family cattle farm with a whole lot of help from Gavin. Curtis decided to make a career as an Army Ranger and only recently retired after eighteen years to take a job with the government doing God knows what.

As for Stone, well – that's a whole other story. One that I'm still not sure about. The only thing that is for certain is that he's not the same kid we knew growing up. The man is more mysterious now than Curtis, who earned the call sign Dark Night because he always came off dark and ominous, hiding in the shadows. Doesn't matter. When it counts, we all know Stone's only a phone call away if we ever need a helping hand. Many times over the last few years, Stone and I have leaned on each other when it came to running our respective ranches like well-oiled machines. Of course, it certainly didn't hurt that Stone seemed to know machinery better than anyone around and loved maintaining them, a trade that I didn't know nearly enough about.

"You may now kiss the bride." Pastor Harold finally announces after what feels like the longest ceremony ever.

Gavin cups Quinn's face in his hands and does just that. The wedding guests all cheer as my best friend and business partner seals the deal on his marriage to the only woman he's ever had eyes for.

Gavin finally lets Quinn come up for air, and the organ starts playing. I'm pulled back to the here and now. The entire church is on their feet as Pastor Harold introduces the newlyweds to the guest, and together they walk hand and hand down the aisle with huge smiles on their faces. I have no doubt that those two have a one-of-a-kind love. The kind of love like my parents have, and Gavin and Quinn's parents. The one that's going to last forever.

When it's my turn, I take my cue, moving to the middle of the alter to link arms with Kinsley June, Quinn's best friend, who is two years younger than the rest of us. She smiles up at me and blushes as she loops her arm in mine. For a split second, I think about potentially hooking up with her after the reception, then swiftly decide against it. Don't get me wrong. Kinsley is pretty fucking hot. She's exactly my type: fun, flirty, not looking for commitment, and I know we're sexually compatible. Trust me, I know. I've been there before with Kinsley have absolutely zero complaints.

The thing is, I want something more. The erratic feeling has been rolling around in my mind for weeks, months even. That restless feeling where you just can't figure out what you want, but you know it's more than what you got.

What the hell is wrong with me? I wish I knew. It's got to have something to do with these damn wedding bells. Surely all the getting married and having babies talk has gotten to me and makes me want to run for the hills to do something crazy.

Regardless, I don't have time to worry about any of that right now.

The rest of the bridal party makes it down the aisle, and we all gather at the back of the church to mingle with the guest while Gavin and Quinn greet everyone with a traditional receiving line. Curtis' fiancée Gidget finds us, and he takes the chance to introduce her to our hometown while they wait in line. I carefully watch the two of them, how they interact together and how Gigi – as she insisted we all call her, seems to fit right in, despite her city girl roots and rich family ties. Together they look content even if there's still that edge to my brother that I can't seem to place, not to mention the daggers that Stone seems to be silently sending him. If Curtis is aware of those daggers, he's doing a damn good job of ignoring them.

Kinsley elbows me, "Why are you frowning?"

"What? Me?" I point at myself. Was I really frowning? *Shit.* I should have a smile plastered on my face and not some damn scowl for whatever fucking reason.

"Yes, you. I thought you'd be thrilled for Gavin and Quinn. Or are you sad because you just lost your drinking buddy?" Kinsley laughs. She's been around enough times to know just how crazy all of us can get.

"I didn't lose a drinking buddy. I gained a designated driver." I joke because it's the truth, and we both know it. Quinn's picked our drunk asses up from Rusty's Tavern quite a few times since they've been together, and never once has she complained.

"You're awful, Day." Kinsley teases.

"What you see is what you get," I wink, and she rolls her eyes.

It takes a solid thirty minutes before the place finally clears out. Then we've all got to hang around for a little bit longer until the photographer has gotten all the formal shots she thinks she needs from us. By the time she's finished with us, my goddamn cheeks hurt from smiling for the camera.

Once she's dismissed us, we all pile out to the small parking lot to get in our vehicles. Gigi and Curtis pile in the back of my truck, and we head back to the farm where we're hosting the reception for the love birds.

All week, in between our regular chores, everyone has worked their asses off to put together one hell of an after-party for Gavin and Quinn, including my twin brother and soon to be sister-in-law who arrived in town and at just the right moment.

Quinn couldn't have picked a better date to get the fall wedding she was looking for.

Set against the stunning fall backdrop of small mountains and farmland for as far as the eye can see, the smaller barn on our property that is usually used for storage has been cleaned out and transformed into what Quinn swears is a cowgirl's dream. and since my best friend only gets married once, I took care of the catering. and I made damn sure everything was running smoothly before I headed to the church earlier while my Mom and Dad promised to watch over everything from there since everyone else would be at the church.

Having everyone *home* sure has been nice, especially having my parents in town. It wasn't too long after I took over things that my parents traded cattle and horses for sunshine and beaches. and since Gavin moved into his new house with Quinn a while back, my childhood home gets a little...lonely sometimes.

Hell, maybe that's why I feel torn between marrying the next girl I see and fucking my way through half the state.

I turn off the main road and head down our gravel driveway, around to the back of the house where we usually park. The minute the truck stops, Curtis hops out and helps Gigi down before mumbling something and rushing off toward the makeshift bar like his ass is on fire. Gigi looks at me and gives me a warm smile and a shrug, brushing off my brother's quick escape.

"You good?"

"Yep."

"I'm telling ya, you sure picked a good one. Curtis can be an ass sometimes."

"Nah. He's got a lot on his mind, is all. Work and everything going on. I don't think I've ever seen him not working. It's probably killing him not being able to log in to his computer and do some top-secret badass stuff." She replies.

"Still, I don't know how you put up with him."

"You're the one who grew up with him." Gigi teases.

"Yeah, and I wanted to kill him a lot of the time." That's only partially true. Curtis and I got along reasonably well. The other half of the time, we were either fighting each other or fighting for each other. I'm pretty sure our mother went prematurely gray because of the two of us.

"I think I'll go find your parents and make sure they don't need anything." Gigi goes on like we're not talking about how my brother is being the weirdest jerk face.

Relationships are weird. Talk about a good reminder of why I've stayed single for so long.

"I'm sure they're around here somewhere." I nod and head for the bridal party tent where we're all supposed to meet up again.

Knowing Gavin, we'll be waiting a while. The classic car he borrowed from his old man hasn't pulled up yet, and the newlywed's house is only a few miles from here. He probably stopped off to consummate his marriage immediately. At the same time, the rest of us suckers have to stand around in our Sunday best and wait on them to show up.

Curtis is standing near the bar in the bridal party tent, downing a glass of amber liquid when I step inside. I join him and order a drink of my own before launching into my little interrogation. If something is up with him, I wanna know.

"Something wrong? You jumped out of my truck like your ass was on fire."

He grunts and swallows back another round.

"Listen, I'm not one to tell you what to do. That said, you might wanna take it easy before you make an ass of yourself. It is Gavin's wedding." I hate that I'm scolding him, but I know how this goes if he has too much to drink. It's been years since Curtis has really tied one on. The last time he did, I ended up with a black eye, and he had a busted lip. I'm sure the bride and groom would really appreciate it if there wasn't any bloodshed at their wedding.

"Just taking the edge off."

"Your next glass should probably be water," I say with a nod to the bartender to make sure he's heard me.

Curtis sighs and concedes, "You're right. Getting drunk isn't going to help matters anyway."

"You keep talking in riddles that make no damn sense."

"Ah, little brother, some things you just wouldn't understand."

This time I chuckle, "Yeah and there you go again. Weirdo. Before you go back to DC, I'm going to get to the bottom of whatever has crawled up your ass."

Part of me wonders if Curtis even remembers what it's like not to be so grumpy and closed off.

Curtis's face pales ever so slightly, given way to whatever façade he's been trying to maintainand just as quickly, his mask slips back into place. "Whatever. Looks like the newlyweds are here."

"Saved by the wedding bells...this time." I tease. At least this time, I get a half-ass smile from him.

TWO
MAEVE

Ping.

The minute I log into the computer from my office, I get an alert for an incoming email. A quick glance tells me that it's from the planning committee for the *No More Sleepless Nights* charity gala coming up.

Just a few short weeks away, the gala is one of the most significant fundraising events for *No More Sleepless Nights*, an organization created to help homeless families in the Washington DC area. The gala brings together all of the who's who of Washington, D.C., for one night to raise money for their cause. With the funds raised, they're able to place homeless families in temporary and permeant housing.

It's always been one of my favorite events to attend alongside my father, Vice Admiral Rodney Peterson. This year, I was given the distinct privilege to help plan the whole thing along with six other notable people from the area. If this event goes well, it can put Peterson Events and Marketing on the map as one of the area's top agencies.

When I started building the company from the ground

up three short years ago, I never thought I'd get to where I am today, but I'm damn proud of how far we've already come. If not for my team of employees, we wouldn't be where we are today. And we wouldn't have the ability to donate our time and energy to this event.

Before I get down to business for the day, I open the event planning committee's email to find that the caterer we booked has suddenly dropped out. They're looking for last-minute recommendations. Two weeks isn't a lot of time to find someone. If we're lucky, someone will have space, so I quickly pull up my vendor information and flip to caterers. A few I already know are booked. I call a few others to ask about availability and cost before compiling a list to email back to the team.

A text message from my best friend rolls in on my phone reminding me that I've also only got two weeks to find a date for said charity gala. I shake my head and type a quick reply letting her know that I'm well aware that I am still painstakingly single and will probably be attending the event alone. Like she has many times before, Adele offers to set me up on a blind date, which I kindly refuse. The last time I went on a blind date, the night ended horribly. I do not wish to have a repeat of that ever again.

It takes a good chunk of my morning to empty my inbox, then begin checking off all the to-dos for events we've got on the books for this weekend. A few of my employees are out of the office at events today and we've got two more lined up for both Saturday and Sunday.

I check in with Autumn, who's handling her first wedding tomorrow, to make sure she's all set and see if she needs any help with last-minute things. Then I field a handful of phone calls from clients.

The rest of the day seems to run smoothly and before I

know it, it's time for me to head out for a Friday evening dinner hosted by a local politician. We've been planning this dinner for his campaign team for months and with election season upon us, we're doing more and more of these.

This one is pretty straightforward. Set at a nearby restaurant, *The Chow,* venue and food are taken care of. My sole job tonight is to make sure all the gift bags for his employees are put together and ensure that everything runs smoothly.

I arrive at *The Chow* an hour before the guests are set to arrive and check over everything. Place settings are good to go with the evening's itinerary set atop the place settings. Each gift bag is put together as it should be and dispersed around the room for the night's attendees. Before long, Congressman Nolan and his team begin filtering in along with the rest of tonight's guests.

"Miss Peterson," Congressman Nolan approaches me and extends his hand. "Things look lovely. Thanks so much for putting this all together for me."

"Good evening, Sir. It's been my pleasure. Everything is good to go."

"Have you met my wife?" he asks and turns to the stunning woman beside him. "Emily, this is Miss Peterson."

"Good evening, Mrs. Nolan. It's so great to meet you," I shake hands with her as well.

"Miss Peterson, this is lovely. It's so great to meet you as well. I've been telling Bob here that I couldn't wait to see what you've done. You know, I'm looking for someone to put together a luncheon for my book club's anniversary. I would love to talk to you more and see if we can't schedule something."

I smile proudly. "That would be wonderful. I'm sure we can make something work."

"Oh, that's so great. Can we chat later tonight?" Mrs. Nolan asks.

"Absolutely."

"You're a darlin'. I appreciate it so much."

Congressman Nolan sweeps his wife away after our brief exchange so they can make their way around the room to greet everyone. I fade into the background and roll up my sleeves to help out wherever I'm needed.

When the evening finally wraps up, I'm exhausted and my feet are killing me. None of that matters when I feel like I'm floating on cloud nine. Everything went off without a hitch. The Congressman and his wife are thrilled with how things turned out.

I exchange numbers with Mrs. Nolan, who promises to call me first thing on Monday to talk about the luncheon she wants to plan before they leave. I hang back until everything is cleaned up to ensure everything is taking care of and nothing has been forgotten. With one last thank you and a final payment to the restaurant, including a hefty tip courtesy of The Nolan's, I'm finally able to go home.

I make a pit stop at my favorite liquor store on the drive home to pick up a bottle of wine. With not one but two bottles of Pinot Noir in hand, I head for the register. Almost to the check-out line, a familiar voice calls out my name. Blood drains from my face, and a chill runs down my spine.

"Maeve, it is really you." I don't even need to look up to see his face. I know exactly who that voice belongs to.

I will not let him see me break. Forcing my shoulders back, I raise my head high and plaster fake confidence on my face.

"Peter." His name rolls off my tongue in disgust.

The man standing before me nearly destroyed my life

and my reputation. The fact that he has the balls to even mention my name is awfully brave of him.

He chuckles nervously, "It's been a while."

"Four and a half years to be exact," I spit the words at him.

The woman beside him looks me over in disgust. *Oh, honey. If you only knew.* Peter Westbrooke is the one she should be disgusted with.

"How have you been?"

"Better without you."

His lips form a tight line. I can almost hear his teeth grinding together, and it's so rewarding right now. Knowing that he no longer holds the power to control me gives me even more courage to stand taller.

"Have you met my *wife?*" The way he says wife is meant to sting. It was a good try on his part, but I'm not phased. Another time, another place, and I would have been destroyed by the notion that he married someone else. The woman I am today – is not.

"I don't believe I've had the pleasure. Funny that Peter never mentioned you before." If he wants to play dirty, I can too.

Blondie's brows arch and her body stiffens as she looks down her nose at me. "How do you two know each other? Work colleagues?"

Aww. Isn't that cute? She thinks we were work colleagues. Hm. I guess you could say that. We did work together at another marketing firm until Peter got me fired when I'd had enough of his bullshit and found out that he was married. I moved from Baltimore to DC after that because I needed a fresh start. I can't say I'm the least bit surprised that these two are in town, though. Peter has several friends in the area who are always hosting parties and such.

Not waiting for Peter to answer her with what I know will be a lie, I tell her the truth. "Well, not exactly. Peter and I dated for a while. That was until I found out he was married. Isn't that right, Peter?"

Steam is practically coming from his ears, and his wife's face turns beet red.

"I think you must be mistaken." She tries to defend her husband.

I almost feel sorry for her.

"Hm. I don't think I am. This has really been fun. Now, if you'll excuse me, I've got someplace else to be tonight."

As I walk away, Peter tries one more time to hit his mark. "I'm sure you can't wait to get back to your apartment and drink that whole bottle of wine, *alone*."

He's good. Real good. The bottle nearly slips from my hand, but I manage to recover and take a deep breath. *I will not let him win.*

The cashier has clearly heard the whole exchange and gives me a warm smile and head nod. "That'll be $46.57."

I hand her fifty dollars and smile right back at her. She mouths, 'I'm sorry,' and I shake my head. I don't need anyone's pity. Even if I'm going home to drink a bottle of wine on my own. Drinking alone sure as hell beats being trapped in a relationship with a narcissistic asshole who claimed to have commitment issues. Guess that worked out well for him with his very pregnant wife.

Not going to let it get to me. At least that's what I keep repeating to myself over and over on the car ride to my apartment. And all night, with each glass of wine I finish.

Fuck Peter and his bimbo baby momma too.

THREE

DAMON

I've spent the entire day working with Gavin's horseback riding clients – something that I haven't done in years. Before he left for his honeymoon, he mentioned that we've got enough interest that we could probably hire another instructor. After today, I think he's right.

Don't get me wrong, things were going great with most of the clients, but the last one of the day indeed takes the cake. This woman is forward. That's for damn sure.

"I bet you would like to tie me to your bedpost," I sigh and roll my eyes at yet another of her come-ons. "You talk to Gavin like this too?"

The perky blonde's eyes widen, and she shakes her head 'no.' "I know he's spoken for. You ever seen Quinn pissed off? I'm not trying to get my ass whooped by his pissed-off ol' lady."

"Jesus Christ, Karen. Then don't talk to me like that either. Have a little respect for everyone around here. This is a business. It's not a dating service."

This time she has the sense to look embarrassed. "I'm

sorry. I heard somethings about you and thought you might be interested, you know?"

I swear, it's been one thing after another since Gavin's wedding and since the bastard left for his honeymoon. Picking up the slack has never been an issue before – then again, neither of us have ever been out of the "office" for more than a day either.

"Like I said, it's a business. I don't know what you heard, but I'm not in the habit of foolin' around with clients. and I'm not about to make an exception." I damn well wasn't given off *interested* vibes either. Hell, all I did was help her tack up the horse. The next thing I know, she wants me to tie her up.

The physical labor is the easy part. It's all this bullshit that Gavin usually does handle, piled on top of my typical workload that's fucked me up this week. Suppliers have clearly lost their damn minds, and Gavin's crew seem to be really pressing their luck with Curtis, who volunteered to fill in some gaps. I'm sure a whole lot of it is just the guys trying to get under his skin and break him in, but trust me, we don't need Curtis to be any grumpier than he usually is. The guys won't listen, though.

Thank fuck Gavin will be back on Monday because I don't know if I can handle one more riding lesson with some clinging young debutant that giggles the entire time, especially when they realize they're working with me instead of my very unavailable riding instructor.

I've got half a mind to take a very long and overdue vacation of my own when Gavin comes back.

"Why don't we go ahead and untack this fella now and get him brushed down?" I offer, doing my best to move this riding lesson along.

I miss only dealing with cattle. They don't tend to

seduce you whenever they get the chance like these damn women on horses do. I'd like to talk to the fucker who thought it was a good idea to diversify the family business... wait, yeah, I'm that fucker.

It takes another thirty minutes before I'm finally free of Karen and her come-ons. One thing is for certain, I'm going to need a cold beer or tonight.

By the time the day is done, I barely manage to drag my sorry ass into the house. Lucky for me, my soon to be sister-in-law is standing in the kitchen preparing something that smells a whole lot like Momma's fried chicken.

"Hey there. Curtis walked in a few minutes before you did. He's already in the shower. You've got some time, too, if you want to wash up before we eat."

"Gigi, I don't know what my brother did to hook you, but I'm sure glad he did. You can stay here any time you want. Don't let him tell you otherwise." I wink at her.

She shakes her head and laughs, "You're only saying that because your mom gave me her secret recipe for fried chicken."

"I knew that's what I smelled." Nostalgia and a twinge of jealousy creep in. It would be a whole lot nicer if I had a woman of my own to come in the door to every night, especially if she knew how to cook.

Before I get too caught up in stupid thoughts again, I excuse myself and head for the master suite that I commandeered and remodeled after Mom and Dad moved to Florida.

Freshly showered and well-fed by Gigi, Curtis and I are both shewed outside with a cooler full of beer and orders to relax and catch up some more.

We're already one beer down when Curtis tosses another piece of wood into the fire pit then grabs a second beer for us both. He passes one to me before he sits back down on the wooden stum that's probably been here since before we were kids. If our parents were here right now, Mom would probably be out here warning us about drinking and playing with fire while Dad joins us, but – they didn't stay long, leaving the day after the wedding. Something about missing all the sunshine and warm weather.

"So, you miss being in the city, or you ready to move back home for good?" I chuck the bottle top into the fire and look over at my brother.

"Well, since you brought it up, I was thinking about hanging around a little bit longer. In fact, I have a proposal for you."

"And there goes my relaxing little evening by the bonfire," I snort.

Curtis's half-cocked ideas never turn out well.

"When's the last time you spent some time away from this place?" he asks.

"Every night, when I go to bed. Sometimes on Sundays when I show up for church."

He chuckles. "That's not what I meant. Have you ever actually taken a vacation? And no, four years in the Navy doesn't count."

"If that's the case, then no, I've never taken a vacation."

That's all Curtis needs to launch into his grand proposal.

"See, you aren't the only one who is married to his work. I can't tell you the last time I've taken a break before now. Gigi and me? We're tying the knot in eight months. I figure what better time for me to take a breather and slow down a little bit. Change things up a little bit before I settle down."

"Sounds an awful lot like a guy who is second-guessing walking down the aisle." I can't help but point out.

"Fuck off. Just because *you* can't make time for a relationship doesn't mean everyone else hates the idea of saying 'I do.'"

"Whatever you say. Go on, I'm listening."

I listen to his entire spiel about shaking things up in silence while I try to process what surely feels like another half-cocked idea. Or maybe I'm hearing things. That's it. I must not have heard him right. There's no way he just said what I think he did.

"Let me get this straight, you want to switch places for a few days?"

While I get the feeling that his proposal has a lot more to do with him than it does with me, the timing couldn't be more perfect. Just when I'm contemplating the meaning of life and all that shit. Leave it to Curtis to catch me while I'm vulnerable. The bastard probably doesn't even realize it.

Curtis shakes his head on confirmation. "A week, or two. Why not? What would it hurt?"

Isn't that the question? What would happen if I stepped back and took a breath for a bit? Didn't I deserve that much?

"What in the hell makes you think switching places is a good idea? Curtis, we're not five. We can't go around foolin' people no more."

He straightens up and looks at me somberly for a beat, then tries to play it off. "I didn't say anything about foolin' anyone," he laughs. "Last time we tried that little Becky Mae wanted to kill us."

"That's because she found exactly why we aren't so identical and was pissed she picked the brother with the short end of the stick," I chuckled to myself, thinking back to the very last time we switched places.

Curtis's dumbass wanted to see if his "friend with benefits" Becky Mae Lawson would notice if I tried to seduce her instead. It was right before we were due to leave for Bootcamp. We were so drunk off our asses that I went along with it, not realizing just how fucked up that little game was though I was damn sure that Becky would notice right away. Curtis, on the other hand, disagreed. Since he dared me to do it – well...I've never been one to back down from a dare. The minute Becky took my pants off, she knew. See, what my twin brother had forgotten about was the tattoo that I snuck out and had done without my parents' permission. It sat proudly on my hip but never saw the light of day. Of course, I wasn't about to tell him that was the real reason why Becky knew the difference between the two of us.

THAT NIGHT, I won $100 from my shithead twin brother. I also got slapped by Becky, and Curtis got an ass-whoopin' from Becky Mae's oldest brother. The only reason why Hunter didn't kick my ass is because I shipped out before he could find me.

"I'm not asking you to pretend to be me, hell you couldn't do my job if your life depended on it." Curtis teases then has the nerve to laugh when I flip him off. "I'm sayin' you work too damn hard, and getting away from here for a while maybe good for you. Go to DC, stay at my place, and enjoy the nightlife a little. Who knows, you might meet someone. Just wash the sheets before you come back home." He pushes the subject some more.

"So, you're just going to take off work? and who's going to take care of everything around here?" I questioned. Curtis seemed to have it all figured out, but I didn't exactly share his confidence.

"I will," he answered, then sighed. "Listen, the truth is, I think we both could use a break. Being back home, it's really made me think about some things, and I'd like a little more time to figure it all out. And you, you're wound so tight these days. So consumed with this place that you haven't even taken a chance to live a little. I don't know, man; I feel like it's time for me to step up and give you a break."

"I don't know what the hell is on your mind or where this need to give me a break is coming from, but you can figure it all your shit out while I'm right here, keeping this place running."

"I can handle things here. You know it, and I know it."

"You mean to tell me; you think you can keep the farm running for what – a week or more? Especially when you haven't been home in what, fifteen or sixteen years? Dude, a few days helping feed the chickens and turning out the horses does not mean you can handle this shit." Maybe I was laying it on a little thick. Deep down, I knew if my brother meant it – he could and would take care of shit here.

Besides, Gavin would be back to help out too, it wasn't like I was leaving the place in incapable hands. But I wouldn't be doing my sibling duty if I didn't act like a little bit of an asshole and fight him on this for a least a few minutes.

Maybe spending some time in the city would be fun. It would certainly be something new to experience. I could literally see how the other half lives.

"I'll make you a deal," the cocky fucker grins. Whatever Curtis was about to say next would no doubt seal my fate. I could feel it. "I've got some vacation time to burn before the end of the year. I'll bet you five grand that I can handle things here for three weeks and that you won't be able to handle not checking in one time in those three weeks."

"I don't need your damn money," I grunt.

"Never said you did, but I happen to know that five grand would go a long way on the repairs for that motorcycle you keep tinkering with but are too cheap to invest any more in because you have this stupid notion that that money could be well spent elsewhere."

Annoyed because he's right, I huff. "I give it three days. You'll have this farm turned upside down and be calling me to come back." I'll be damn if I would going to go down without a fight.

Curtis smirks. "Does that mean we have a deal?"

I stand and hold out my hand. Of course, we have a deal. The motherfucker came for my pride, knowing I wouldn't back down. "You're on."

Gigi walks down off the back porch just after I've slapped Curtis on the back and joins us. "Oh, God. Did you two just make a bet?"

Throwing my head back, I howl out a laugh. "Christ, she's already got us figured out, man. This girl's a keeper."

and there it is again. The tiny flicker in Curtis's eyes and the slight flinch. That whole twin ESP thing was happening though I couldn't put my finger on exactly what was going on. and if Curtis wasn't ready to open up to me, well, then wasn't anything I could do about it except keep giving him good-natured hell for his brainy ideas.

"Day's going to spend some time at the townhouse. Figured a little extension to our vacation here on the farm might be nice."

I half expect my soon to be sister-in-law to bulk at the idea of a prolonged stay in Bitterhill, she is a true city girl after all, but she doesn't even blink. "Hmm. With everything coming up, I think that's a great idea. Damon may even fall in love with the city! I've got a single friend. I could call her up and ask her to show you around." She winks at me.

"Thanks, Gi, but I'm quite alright on my own." I shake my head. "You two love birds okay our here with the fire if I head on inside for the night?"

"Damon, I know how to handle a damn campfire. Go to bed." Curtis grumbles at me.

"Well then, goodnight to you both." I grab the empty beer bottles and carry them back to the house with me to toss in the recycling.

If I was really going to DC, I would need to pack and make a list of things to take care of before I left. Christ, now that I agreed to this nonsense, I felt like my head was spinning. Two or three weeks of blind faith felt like a lot, even if I knew I'd have the two best people on the job.

Maybe I could convince Gavin to send me updates and send a few friends to check in on things.

Yup, that's exactly what I'll do. First thing tomorrow, I'll give Stone a call him that I need a favor too. For now, I was going the hell to bed because that damned old rooster crowed early.

FOUR
MAEVE

Finally finished reviewing color swatches and dessert options with my last client for the day, I shut my computer down and log out before spinning around in my chair and staring out the third story office window that overlooks the heart of DC. Evening traffic has already started to die down, and the entire city is lit up. It's like a beacon to my heart.

You would think that being a Navy brat would mean moving lots of places over the years, but the fact that my mother walked out on us when I was just a year old meant my father was on his own. Thankfully, his sister, my Aunt Tillie, stepped in and took care of me whenever Dad was deployed. That meant I grew up in the city my entire life, no matter where my father was stationed.

First, it was Baltimore, then Washington, DC. This used to be the only place I thought of as home. Now that I was running my own event planning company, Dad was in DC for the foreseeable future. There was no need to travel to visit him – I had to admit that I feel like something's missing. Something that I kept trying to tell myself had nothing to do with running into my ex last week.

After Peter, I swore off men for a long time. There were a few casual dates here and there, thanks to some well-meaning friends, but nothing ever went further than a handful of dates or a one night stand or two.

Nope. The itch I was feeling had nothing to do with Peter and everything to do with a heart that was lonely long before Peter and I broke up.

With a deep breath, I roll my shoulders to relieve the mounting tension that was amplified the minute Marcus Wrigley's name flashed on my caller id. Between the sour mood I'd been in since seeing Peter again and dealing with all of Marcus' demands, I could feel a headache coming on. The flamboyant playboy gave all of my past clients a run for their money with his list of demands. Thankfully, I got precisely what Marcus wants at the end of the day, and his wedding is set to go off without a hitch this weekend.

Everyone else in my office has headed out, and it's way past my usual quitting time. Which means, if I'm still going to make it to my regular Thursday night visit to *Sit & Sip*, I'm going to need to get a move on.

The *Sit & Sip* is surprisingly quiet when I walk in fifteen minutes later. My favorite bartender, Justin, is behind the bar and spots me when I step in the door. Before I even pull up a stool, he's got my favorite IPA in a glass and waiting for me.

"Long week?" he asks.

"Wasn't too bad until around two o'clock this afternoon."

He laughs. "Let me guess, another Bridezilla who couldn't find the right shade of bubblegum pink for her napkins?"

I snort and shake my head. "Something like that."

Justin's known me since I turned twenty-one. He's been

there with me through being fired from the last event planning company I worked for to starting my own. Every lousy breakup and every funny mishap, I've shared them all with Justin and his wife Marcie - a flight attendant for one of the biggest airlines in the US.

"Where's everybody at tonight?"

"New upscale cocktail bar opened a few blocks away. Looks like everyone is trying it out tonight." Justin shrugs.

Sit & Sip has been here for as long as I can remember. This isn't the first new bar that's popped up and won't be the last. *Sit & Sip* has always prevailed, and I have no doubt that they will once more, which is exactly why Justin doesn't seem to be bothered by the slower than normal night.

"Chicken tenders or a burger?" Justin asks while wiping down the bar top.

I laugh because he knows me so well. I don't think I've ever left here without eating some sort of very late dinner. "Hm. I think I'll do the chicken tenders today."

"Extra honey mustard?"

"Oh, you know it," I answer with a smile.

Justin gives me a cheesy wink. "Coming right up."

While he puts in my food order, I check a few messages and scroll through my social media.

Friends, colleagues, they're all posting pictures of themselves out on the town. Or pictures of their cute little families. and then there's me, sitting in the corner bar – alone, on a Thursday night. Peter's words run through my head again. It all amounts to one thing...*alone*. I'm alone.

All the time I spent growing my firm didn't leave much room for anything else after we broke up. I buried myself in work because Peter said I'd never make it. I don't regret working hard, even if it was an excuse to keep my mind off my personal life. But now, for some reason, I feel like I'm missing out.

Do I really want to settle down? Do I want that happily ever after? Doesn't every little girl dream of it? Right now, I'd settle for just a little male connection.

The Love Bites dating app taunts me from my apps screen on my phone. I downloaded the app months ago when I needed a date for an event with some high profile people. I created a profile, got one round of matches, and never really touched it after that because all of the guys seemed to be looking for hookups. That wasn't what I wanted then. Maybe now it was time to revisit things if nothing more than to have a little fun and scratch a long overdue itch.

It's not like I've got anything to lose.

Click.

The app loads quickly, and I'm startled by the outdated messages from the last and only time I logged in. I delete those and hit the re-match button. Several new photos pop up, and I begin scrolling through profiles until I land on what seems like the perfect match.

Damon

Age: 36

Current Location: NW DC

His profile is straightforward, and the photos he's attached check off every single box for me.

This is someone I'd have fun with, I mumble to myself.

"Oooh. Love Bites," Justin chuckles as he sets my food down. "Good for you."

Startled by him, I nearly drop by phone and accidentally click match. "Shit. Well, you've gone and done it now, Justin."

He shrugs. "Change is good."

"Yeah, well. Who says I was ready for a change?" I sigh nervously. "I was just pursuing my options. He probably won't even respond anyway."

"He'd be a fool not to."

"You're only saying that because I tip well." I joke, but at least Justin's always been on my team.

"Girl, seriously. When's the last time you went out on a date? I know you're content, and that's fine. No judgment whatsoever. Remember, you do deserve a little fun and happiness in your life."

I don't have a chance to reply to Justin. Another patron walks in, and he moves down the bar to wait on them.

Ignoring the app, for now, I pop a fry in my mouth and enjoy my second glass of beer with my meal. We'll see what happens. If nothing else, maybe I'll get laid.

Chicken tenders and one more beer finished, I decide it's time for me to head home and get some rest. Tomorrow will be busy, and I've got plenty of last-minute errands to run for Marcus' wedding.

Justin closes out my tab and insists on walking me home, letting his assistant manager fill in for him.

"You know I can really walk home by myself," I tell him on the short walk.

"I know you *can,* but what kind of pseudo big brother would I be if I *let* you?" He nudges my side.

I guess you could say that Justin adopted me the first time I walked into his bar all those years ago.

"I think it's more a matter of the fact that you know Marcie wouldn't be happy with you if you let her best friend walk home alone."

He mocks offense and scoffs at me. "Okay, well, that's true too, but I'd do it for anyone, and you know it."

"You're right. You would," I playfully pat Justin's cheek

when we stop outside my apartment building. "Thank you for making sure I got home safely."

"Anytime."

Justin waits while I make my way inside. By the time I let myself into my apartment and check the window, he's gone, and I'm left to my own devices, which I think might just include a bubble bath and a good book.

FIVE
DAMON

My first night in DC certainly wasn't one for the record books, but not having to get out of bed with the sunrise is.

Taking full advantage of the fact that I have nowhere to be and nothing to do, I roll over and grab my cell phone that was charging on the nightstand to check for any missed calls. I made Gavin swear that he'd keep me in the loop and let me know if I needed to make a surprise appearance to take care of anything. What can I say? Old habits die hard. I feel like I've left my child with someone for the first time, and admittedly, I'm nervous about it.

There are no messages or missed calls, which is a good sign since they all should be well into their tasks for the day back home. Before I put the phone down, I notice an alert on the Love Bites app that I installed on a whim last night after one too many beers.

"Good Lord, what was I thinking?" I say out loud to the empty space around me, but I already know exactly what I was thinking. It's been months since my last hook up and even longer since my previous relationship. After a six-pack of beer and the greasiest pizza in town, I decided it was a good idea to break my dry spell and see what DC women had to offer. Why not, right? I'm only in town for a little bit, and this app promised to match me with women who were just looking to have fun. Last night, I thought I had nothing to lose.

Call me a man whore all you want, who hasn't ever had a little fun, right?

One click on the match results and I'm immediately taken back by the beautiful woman on the screen.

Maeve

Age: 29

Currently Location: NW DC

Her bio says she's an entrepreneur looking for fun and short-term companionship. Married to her job and not looking for a long-term commitment.

Clearly, coming to DC means there's a first time for everything. This whole thing is so far out of my norm that I almost question if I've lost my mind.

Before I talk myself out of it, I quickly hit accept to her match request and type out a quick message inviting her to meet up over coffee. Then I leave the rest up to fate and decide that I owe it to myself to take an actual day of relaxation, starting with more sleep.

When I wake up again around eleven, I crawl out of my twin brother's oversized bed and head for the shower. Hot water blasts my body from damn near every angle, and while I'd normally call this overkill – and I still swear that Curtis must have more money than brains – I am thoroughly enjoying this slice of luxury at the moment. Add taking a long hot shower to the list of things I don't do often enough. Usually, I'm only in the shower long enough to take care of business and move on to the next task or curl up in bed for the night.

My cell phone is ringing when I come walking back into the bedroom with a towel around my waist. Gavin's number flashes on the screen, and I quickly swipe to answer.

"Everything's fine; you can take a breath." He chuckles on the other end.

"Fuck you, man. Has Curtis quit yet?"

"Nah, Dark Knight is still out there busting his ass. I've gotta say, I'm impressed too. Who knew he still had it in him?"

"Yeah, well, tell the fucker not to get too comfortable doing my job. This isn't a permanent arrangement."

"Oh, I don't think he's going to be replacing you anytime soon. That's why I was calling. Before you ask, we don't need you to come home. But Gigi couldn't hang, apparently. She left this morning, and now, shew whee, your brother is in a hell of a mood. I just thought you should know."

"So, you do need me to come home." I sigh. I can only imagine what the dumbass did to set his fiancée off.

"Nope, we're good. Really. I just wanted to give you a heads up for whenever you talk to him. Thought he might need a friend." Gavin tells me.

"You wanted to gossip and want me to poke the bear. Now I got it. I'll call his ass and see what's up. That doesn't mean I'm telling you what's going on with him, so stop acting like a girl."

"Alright. Well, you do that. I'm heading to the diner for my lunch, then I need to get back to work. My boss is a real asshole." He ignores my dig about gossiping.

"Fuck off," I laugh. "Thanks for the heads up."

I hang up with Gavin and immediately dial Curtis' phone. It rings a handful of times. Then he finally answers, sounding like he's angry at the world.

"Ah, there's the brother I know and love."

"What do you want? I know you're not calling to ask me how it's going already."

"Nope. I was just calling to tell you that I refuse to pay for your water and utilities while I'm here. and I can't be held responsible for emptying the water tank every time I shower."

"It's a tankless water heater. If you run out of hot water, we've got a big problem. Heads up that Gigi is back in DC. She'll probably try to stop by at some point and get some of her things. She can take whatever."

"Not a fan of country living?" I pry.

"Something like that."

"I thought she lived *here*. Does she need her space back? I can come home."

"Nah. Gigi's got her own apartment. Don't worry about it, seriously."

"You sure? This was all your idea. I'm happy to come back home if things have changed."

"Listen, I'm sure. Just let it be, would ya? I think the time away from each other will be good for us. Just leave it at that and be kind to her if she stops by for some of her things."

Something tells me that Curtis isn't totally honest with me. As much as I want to keep poking him, I know if I do, he's only going to shut down on me. "Alright, I'm leaving it alone. I'm here if you need me."

Curtis huffs, "No offense, *little* brother, I've been handling my shit on my own for a long time. I've got this. But thanks."

"Whatever, grumpy. Don't be an ass to everyone else just because you won't be getting laid for a few weeks."

"Fuck off, Day. Go get into some trouble or something.

There's a strip club on the far side of town that's pretty nice. Maybe check it out."

"Go to hell," I chuckle. I've only been to a strip club once. The boys scored fake IDs before I left for the Navy and took me out for what they called one last hoorah. Not sure I'd ever want to go back to a place like that. Then again, not all strip clubs are the same, or so I'm told. "I'll talk to you later."

Before I set my phone down, I notice there's another alert from the Love Bites app. Half-heartedly hoping that it's the woman who matched with me, I open it up.

Forget coffee. I'm going out with friends tonight, why don't you meet me at The Warehouse at 9pm?

Here's my number...

Looks like I officially have plans tonight.

SIX

MAEVE

I must admit, I'm pleasantly surprised when Damon accepts my offer to meet me at *The Warehouse*. When he mentioned coffee, I thought for sure he'd balk going to a club, but part of me felt like it would be much safer if I met him with my friends around. Plus, it would hopefully keep me from feeling like a third with Zeke and Adele.

I'm sure those two would freak if they knew that I felt that way, but they're newlyweds and madly in love with one another. I can't blame them for never being able to keep their hands to themselves. It does make for some awkward situations, and it's the reason why I haven't ventured out with them for a bit. Damon gave me the perfect excuse. and if he doesn't show up, well, I still got my ass out of the apartment for a while and had a chance to unwind after a fabulous event for Marcus that went off without a hitch.

We get to the club at eight, which is early enough that Adele and I have plenty of time to warm up out on the dance floor, and I can shake off my pre-date jitters. By the time nine o'clock rolls around, we've danced a few songs and already thrown back the first two rounds of drinks. I quickly check my phone to make sure I didn't miss Damon's message, then scan the club to see if I can spot him. When I don't see his face in the crowd, I excuse myself and head for the restroom.

I check my phone one more time for good measure on the way, only to collide with a solid wall of muscle and stumble, nearly losing my balance.

Two strong arms wrap around me to stop me from falling backward. A tiny jolt of sparks from the stranger's touch shocks my body, sending a shiver down my spine. I'm captivated by the most amazing turquoise eyes that I've ever seen when I look up. It takes a minute for my brain to process before I let out a nervous giggle when I realize who I've just collided with. "Damon?"

He smiles, and two tiny dimples appear, making my insides swoon.

"I'm taking it that you're Maeve," he says over the music.

"You found me. I was just heading to the restroom." I offer in explanation, fighting back a case of butterflies from the sparks that I feel like are flying around us.

"Oh, go ahead, I'll wait," he extends an arm to let me pass by. I instantly miss the contact.

"I'll just be a minute," I call out over my shoulder.

I relieve my bladder, wash my hands, and splash some cold water on my face. It must be the alcohol that causing the blush on my cheeks. There's no way it has anything to do with the man I just met, I try to tell myself.

True to his word, Damon is leaning against the wall, waiting for me when I return.

"My friends are right over there," I point to the corner table where Zeke and Adele are lost in each other's gaze. He gives me a nod and loops my arm in his as we make our way across the room. I tap on the table to get their attention and introduce my friends to my date for the evening.

Damon's eyes widen in surprise, "Zeke...Zeke Hadley?"

Zeke shakes his head in disbelief and stands. "Fuck if it isn't Damon Knightly, in the flesh."

"You two know each other?" I ask.

"We do, actually. Damon and I served together in the Navy, what nineteen years ago or so?" Zeke explains.

"Something like that, yeah. It's been that long. Have you retired yet?" Damon asks.

Disappointment hits me. This is what I get for trying my luck on some stupid dating app. I'm willing to bet Damon will spend the whole night talking guy shit with Zeke, and I'll still be the third goddamn wheel anyway. Plus, it sounds like he's military. I make it a point to never get involved with a man in uniform.

Zeke laughs. "I did. Took some time to do some traveling and met this gorgeous woman. We got married six months ago."

Damon shakes Adele's hand and congratulates both of them. "Fuck, you still look exactly the same man. I can't believe of all places...wow."

"I'd recognize that face of yours anywhere, but I gotta say, you're a hell of a lot bigger than your scrawny ass was at eighteen."

"Oh, please. I could still bench more than you in training," Damon laughs.

While they catch up, I take a minute to soak Damon in from head to toe. If I'm going to be stuck here all night, I might as well enjoy the view. I already suspected he wasn't from DC. The dark wash Wranglers, Texas-sized belt buckle, and Cowboy boots confirm it. The dark gray polo shirt that he's wearing might as well be painted on, and I'm only remotely shocked that he's not wearing a pearl snap button-down instead.

Damon turns to me and pulls me into their conversation. "So, how long have you known these two?"

"A few years. They live in my apartment building." I eye them both and giggle to myself when they both flush red.

"Oh shit, sounds like there's a story there."

"There is one heck of a story about how we met. Should I tell him?" I bat my eyes and tease Zeke and Adele.

Adele shakes her head, and Zeke tries to stop me. "I don't think that's necessary."

"Aww, come on. It's a funny story."

"This sounds like something I gotta know," Damon eggs me on.

"Nope. Not a word," Adele hisses.

"Fine," I hold my hands in up surrender. "I won't tell him."

Damon fakes a pout and changes the subject, this time focusing on me.

Okay, so maybe I was wrong about him. Right now, he's looking at me like I'm the only person in the room. I have to take a sip of my drink before I can even speak because he's made my mouth go dry with his penetrating stare.

I've never been good at small talk, so my best attempt comes out, making me feel dorky and awkward. I'm entirely off-kilter. "So, Damon, what brings you to DC?"

"A stupid bet with my twin brother."

I nearly choke on the beer I just swallowed. "There are two of you that look like that?" I wave a finger up and down. A million and one thoughts run through my head, some PG, the others not so much.

Damon chuckles and leans in as if he can read my mind, "I'll let you in on a little secret. I'm the better choice."

"I bet you are," I laugh and feel some of my anxiousness dissolve away. "What exactly was this bet about?"

"Long story short, he seems to think I won't make it two weeks in the city. I'm betting he won't make it two weeks on the family farm."

"So, you're swapping lives, like that movie – *The Parent Trap*." *Way to go with the lame movie reference, Maeve.*

Damon grins and shakes his head. "No, not exactly. I think he got the raw end of the deal. I'm taking a vacation of sorts while I'm in town, and he's taking over my job. We're not fooling anyone, I promise."

"So, you're really Damon, and he is...?"

"Curtis, though everyone calls him Dark Knight. He's the dark and broody one of the bunch."

"Hm. Are you're the life of the party?"

"Something like that." His smile widens, showcasing those sexy dimples again.

"and are *you* still in the Navy, or did you retire?"

"Uhm. Neither. I did four years out of high school, then came back home."

"Nothing wrong with that. Last question...tell me something, Cowboy, do you know how to dance?" I raise a questioning brow.

"I might. Are you fixing to find out?"

"What's the point of being here if we're not going to dance a little?" I slide off my stool and take his hand. "What do you say, Cowboy?" I give him a tug toward the dance floor.

He doesn't resist. Instead, he takes the lead and finds an empty spot on the dance floor just as the DJ begins playing *The Git Up* by Blanco Brown. The club erupts in a cheer around us, and at first, I'm worried that he'll be able to keep up but damn, if this hot cowboy doesn't bust out some of the smoothest moves I've ever seen. I'm in absolute awe. If he notices all the women watching him, he doesn't pay a moment of attention to any of it. His gaze is locked on me until the very last beat.

The Git Up transitions to *Hands on Your Knees* by Renni Rucci and Kevin Gates. Damon grabs my hand and pulls me closer to him while maintaining a little space between us. As one song melds into another, our bodies move closer until we're pressed against each other. That spark from early is back with a vengeance. Damon moves in tune with the music and with his hands doing their own seductive dance on my body, holding me close while taking my breath away.

I don't know how long we're on the dance floor, but when a slower song finally comes on, we both break away, breathless and in need of a drink.

The sexy smirk on his face as he orders another round is priceless. I can tell that underneath it all, he's a cocky fucker. Damn, if I don't like it. "How's that for a cowboy?" He leans in to whisper in my ear, his lips brushing against my skin, lighting me on fire.

"I'm impressed. I didn't think they taught moves like that on a farm."

The grumble of laughter from his chest vibrates through my body. "I've got plenty of moves," he says with a wink.

Oh, I'm sure you do, I think to myself, knowing that I'd give anything to see them all right now.

SEVEN

DAMON

It's been a long time since I've closed down a bar, yet here I am standing outside some club in DC, waiting for my keys from the valet while Zeke, Adele, and Maeve all wait for their car service to pull up.

There's just one problem, I'm not ready for the night to end.

Maeve has me wound up tighter than I've ever felt before. From her body grinding against mine onthe dance floor to the sexy as fuck kiss she laid on me when I walked her to the bathroom before closing time, she's managed to set my body on fire.

I want to take her home and worship every curve of her body. Explore every inch of her until she forgets her name and is begging for more.

Clearing my throat, I reach for her hand and pull her in closer. It's been a long damn time since I asked a woman to come back to my place, and it's never been someone I didn't know. Maeve is different, though. Something about her has captivated me, putting me under a spell that only she can break.

Feeling awkward as fuck, I find the balls to ask, "Can I invite you back to my place?" while praying I haven't misread the entire night. I can't think of anything worse right now than being embarrassed in front of Zeke while I make a complete fool of myself.

Maeve looks up at me with a gentle smile that makes it hard to tell if she's playing hard to get. "Maybe some other time, Cowboy. I've got an early morning ahead of me."

"Darlin', I'm used to getting up early. Besides, who said anything about sleeping?" I give her a knowing look to be sure that my intentions are obvious.

She gives me an eye-roll, then traces her fingers over my chest and bits her lip with a low hum only I can hear. "Hmm. Is that a promise?"

I take her hand and kiss her fingertips, "That depends. Do you want me to promise to keep you up all night?"

"Yes, please," she purrs. I feel like I now know for sure that the chemistry I've been feeling isn't all one-sided.

"Then it's a promise."

"Adele, Zeke, I'm going to let Damon take me home." She tells her friends just as my truck rolls to a stop in front of us.

Adele quickly hugs her and whispers something that sounds a whole lot like, "Go get 'em, tiger," while Zeke slaps me on the back. "Keep in touch. Let's catch a game or something while you're in town," he tells me.

"Yeah, for sure. I'll give you a call." I promise him as I slide my hand onto the small of Maeve's back.

I trade my keys for a tip to the valet then help Maeve into the passenger side.

"This suits you," she tells me as I climb into the driver's side.

"What does?"

"The truck. Certainly fits your image."

I can tell by the tone in her voice that she's teasing me, so I play along. "You got a problem with my truck? Or my image?"

"Absolutely not," she replies while reaching over the center console and trailing her fingers over my thigh.

Thank fuck, it's a short drive because Maeve can't seem to keep her hands to herself, and I can't find the common sense to stop her when she cups my hard-on through my jeans. The urge to buck into her hand is uncontrollable and only encourages her to continue. By the time we pull up outside Curtis' townhouse, my resolve has just about broken. If it would have taken any longer, I may have ended up embarrassing myself or running off the road.

Somehow, I manage to park, get us both inside, *and* the door locked up behind us before clothes start flying off.

We've barely made it out of the foyer and into the living room before Maeve is completely naked and my pants are around my ankles. I don't have time to appreciate the view before me or even remove my boots and pull my pants the rest of the way because the vixen drops to her knees and has my cock in her mouth without a second thought.

Maeve sucks me from root to tip, letting my cock hit the back of her throat before her hand wraps around my shaft and works in time with her hot little mouth.

"Goddamn," I hiss as my eyes roll back in my head. Things are barely getting started, and I'm already fighting to hang on to every ounce of control. Counting backward doesn't help. Thinking of farm chores isn't enough. Nothing can distract me from the feeling of her mouth on me. I'm tumbling straight toward the point of no return, and there isn't a damn thing I can do to stop it.

She sucks me harder and rolls my balls through her

fingers, moving even faster when I push her hair back from her forehead and fuck her face. Maeve hums around me, and I can feel my balls tighten. My body starts tingling, ears ringing and my heart pumping in double time. I'm not going to be able to hold back for much longer.

I hit the back of her throat again, seeing stars. "Jesus Christ," I try to moan out a warning to Maeve and pull back, but it comes out as a strangled cry of pleasure that is too little too late. I'm full-on throbbing into her mouth while she's taking everything I've got to give with a single swallow before releasing me with a pop that echoes in the space around us.

"Come 'ere." I somehow manage to say out loud. Maeve takes my hands and lets me help her up off the floor. The proud look on her face tells me that she's quite pleased with herself, and she should be. I don't know where the hell she learned to do that, nor do I want to, but I sure as fuck enjoyed it.

Cupping her face in my hands, I kiss her with everything I've got. "Fucking, amazing," I tell before slipping my tongue past her lips. When she groans and rubs against me, I grab her under her ass and scoop her up in my arms. Her wet pussy brushes across my still sensitive cock, eliciting an almost painful hiss from me. I'm already wishing I was buried deep inside her, fucking her brains out and sending her over the edge into oblivion. The sooner I can make that happen, the better.

Completely forgetting that my pants are still around my ankles, I attempt to carry her to the nearest flat surface. Needless to say, we don't make it very far before I stumble and almost fall with her in my arms. She lets out a loud squeal and holds on tighter. Thankfully I'm able to keep us both from landing on the hardwood floor.

"Gimme one second," I grumble in frustration, disappointed that I have to let her go so I can rectify that situation. Maeve giggles while I curse and fumble my way out of what's left of my clothes. But when I look up, she stops and licks her lips.

"Honey, if you keep looking at me like that, I'm going to have to take you hard and fast," I warn her.

"You act like that's a bad thing. Aren't you the one who said we'd be doing this all night?" Maeve challenges me.

If she wants to play, then we'll play.

In a split second, I'm on her, and I fuse my lips to hers. I've got plenty of pent up energy that I'm more than happy to spend worshiping her body. I had plans to carry her sexy as sin body to the bedroom, but I'm thinking that bending her over the couch first is a better option. Or maybe spreading her out on the nearby kitchen table is a better idea. I could feast on her pussy then fuck her senseless.

Being the equal opportunity lover that I am, I slowly back her into the dining area until she bumps into the table. Then I lay her back and spread her legs so that I'm standing between them. She's already begging me to fuck her while I kiss my way down her body, and she squirms under my touch. The table is the perfect height for me to kneel, bury my head between her thighs, and swipe my tongue against her sensitive flesh.

Determined to drive her insane, I take my time before I finally circle her clit then suck on it. Maeve's back arches off the table, and she lets out the sexiest sound. When I add two fingers to the mix, her head begins thrashing side to side while she calls out my name.

While I finger her pussy, I reach up with my free hand and pinch one nipple between my fingers until it's rock hard, then I move to the other side. Maeve pants, begging for more.

It doesn't take long before her body begins to quiver, and her pussy clenches around my fingers. One twist in the right direction, and she screams in pleasure. Her hands dig into my hair, nails scraping against my scalp as she claws her way through her first orgasm.

"Damon!" Her hips flex again, but this time I hold her down with one hand, and she digs her heels into my shoulders. "Holy. Fuck."

Sure that she's been thoroughly taken care of, I begin running my hands up her legs and slowly trace every curve of her body first with my fingers, then following up with gentle kisses.

"More," she mumbles as I kiss her lips. "I need more D. I need all of you."

My cock jumps at the thought, and I'm about to give us both what we want when the lusty haze clears enough to stop me from doing something stupid. "Condom," I grunt, hoping like hell that my asshole twin has some stashed somewhere around here. I hadn't exactly gotten around to buying any because this wasn't the plan.

Maeve nearly knocks me over, scurrying from the table. "In my clutch," she offers as an explanation.

Seconds later, she's produced an entire row of condoms from her little black wallet thing that I'm guessing is this clutch she's speaking of. She quickly tears one off and rips it open with her teeth while tossing the rest on the coffee table. Then my cock is back in her hands, and I'm holding back a groan as Maeve rolls the latex over my shaft.

"Well, don't just stand there," she purrs and bends over the arm of the sofa and shakes her perfect round ass at me.

Christ. This woman is a vixen. Something tells me that

if I'm not careful, Maeve may damn well be the death of me.

I give her ass a slap while rubbing my cock between her legs, then ease my way insider her. Her pussy is like a vice, so tight that it's *almost* painful. The pleasure is so overwhelming and consuming that I have to stand still for a moment to gain some semblance of composure. She doesn't give me a chance for that. Maeve rocks her body back against me.

The need for satisfaction between the two of us shatters my resolve and has me slamming inside her over and over again. At the same time, she pants and calls out my name.

Leaning over her, I pull her hair back over her shoulder and fist it in my hand to give it a gentle tug that causes Maeve to moan and tighten around me.

"Harder," she pants, moving with me on every thrust.

Sweat beads on my forehead as I slam inside her even harder. Keeping her hair wrapped in one hand, I find her clit with the other.

"Damon. Please...oh God, please...yes, yes, yes."

I kiss the side of her neck then give her a nip. "Let go, baby. Come for me." I need her to, more than I need my next breath.

She leans back further and wraps her hands around the back of my neck. "Fuccccck."

The arch of her body changes the friction between us, and Maeve gives in, which sends my eyes rolling back in my head as her body hums around me. There is no more holding back. I follow her over the edge with one final thrust. She's putty in my hands while I try to keep us both upright even though my entire body feels like rubber bands. I can't think of a time when sex was ever this good, this...different.

Once I'm sure that we can both stand on our own, I untangle myself and remove the condom to toss in the kitchen trash can. Pulling open the fridge, I grab us both a bottle of water to drink and offer one to her.

She takes a long drink before finding the words to speak. "Please tell me there is more where that came from."

A wicked grin spreads across my face, "Oh, there is plenty where that came from."

I promised her a sleepless night, and if I have it my way, I'm going to do so much more than keep her up all night. There's a piece of me that wants to consume her. To own every inch of her body and soul.

I've waited thirty-seven years for a woman that can handle all of me. I can't quite put my finger on it, and I never thought I was one that believed in fate, but something tells me that I've finally met my match.

EIGHT

MAEVE

One thing I can say with certainty is that Damon doesn't break promises.

Oh no. Not at all. The man delivered in so many ways. There isn't a surface in this place that hasn't been touched and not a muscle in my body that hasn't been pushed to the limits. Even my face hurts from...well, from a whole lot of action.

I can't remember the last time I saw a sunrise. and I can add "fucked on a rooftop patio where anyone could see exactly what we were doing" to the list of things I never thought I'd do. For the record, though, I'd damn well do it again, especially with Damon. Every inhibition I thought I had has gone out the window. With Damon, I feel free and safe. Which an odd combination that I'm not really ready to analyze, considering I haven't had my morning coffee...

"Shit. Shit, shit, shit, shit..." I push back on Damon's chest and jump up from the lounge chair that we were just cuddling on. "What time is it?"

I'll worry about the fact that I was cuddling... *cuddling, what in the world*...with him later. Much later.

Damon bolts up and checks the only thing he's wearing. Thank God it's a watch. "A little after seven, why? What's wrong?"

"I'm going to be so late, and my Dad is going to kill me." I beeline for the patio door and rush back inside the three-store townhouse to focused on hurrying to worry about the insanely concerned look on Damon's face. Don't get me wrong, I do feel bad, but if I don't leave here in the next few minutes, I will be even later. "My clothes. Where the hell are my clothes?"

He doubles over in laughter.

"This isn't funny!" I try hard not to laugh too, but it's hard not to. I imagine we both look pretty ridiculous right now.

"It is funny. You scared the shit out of me for two seconds when I thought you were going to say something like you needed to get home to your husband or boyfriend."

I stop for a split second and stare him down. "Really, Damon?"

"Sorry. I'm sorry. Your freaking out freaked me out." He's still laughing at me.

"Whatever. Help me find my clothes, damnit!"

"Downstairs," Damon replies, two steps ahead of me.

He helps me gather my things while I rush to put them on. "Ugh! There is no way I can wear this to breakfast. I'm going to have to go home and change."

"Wait." Damon wraps his arms around me to slow me down. "Take a deep breath. Maybe I can find something in my brother's closet. I'm sure his fiancée has some clothes here; she might have something you can borrow."

"Your brother's fiancée? Lives here?" I shake my head. "You know what it doesn't matter. I should just go before I'm any later."

"Woman." He silences me with a quick kiss that has me freezing in place. Damn, he is good at that. "Let me help you. It's the least I can do since it's sort of my fault you're going to be late."

Damon has a point, and if I don't have to rush home to change, I can save some time. God, please let his soon to be sister-in-law have something that works for breakfast with the Vice-Admiral.

"Fine. But seriously, hurry." I push him back toward the stairs that lead to the bedroom and follow quickly behind him.

Thank God for small miracles. It appears the woman has similar taste in fashion and a similar-sized waistline. While I button up the light pink blouse, Damon's eyes remain focused on me, heating my entire body. The black boxer briefs he's wearing do nothing to hide the rather large erection that I'm all too well acquainted with.

"Are you ever not...hard?" I mumble to myself, but the bastard hears me and laughs.

"This is all your fault. It's like I can't turn it off." He replies smugly.

Did I mention he's quite the smooth talker?

Talk about a gentleman in public and one filthy, dirty-talking, sex machine behind closed doors.

"I'm pretty sure I would never get anything done with you around." I sigh. "I need to call for a ride. Damnit. I should have done that while I was getting ready. You don't happen to have a spare toothbrush around here, do you?"

"Hell if I know, but I'll go check." He wanders into the master bathroom while I pull out my phone and queue up an Uber. "Found one," he calls out.

Sure enough, he's located a toothbrush still in the package and set it on the counter for me.

"I'll give you a minute," Damon says as I walk in behind him. He starts to leave, then stops and spins on his heels only to cup my face and kiss me senseless again.

I melt into him and cling to his bare chest while wishing my clothes would disintegrate. I can't get enough of this man. When he finally lets me go, I'm breathless, panting, and about to cancel breakfast with my father just to let Damon feast on me instead.

He smacks my ass and gives me a wink. "You're going to miss your ride if you don't hurry."

"Asshole." I grumble and watch his backside as he walks away.

Teeth brushed and hair pulled up into a halfway decent bun, I walk out of the bathroom and find Damon dressed in basketball shorts and a t-shirt. Disappointment and relief flood me instantaneously. His naked form is far too tempting, but seeing him all covered up should be a sin.

"All set?"

I shake my head, "Yep, this is as good as it's going to get, I'm afraid."

"You look great. I think you'll be fine." He tells me.

"I appreciate the vote of confidence," I reply while checking the status of my Uber on the phone. "My ride should be here any minute, so I better get going."

Damon walks me to the front door like a gentleman. "I had fun. Thanks for staying the night."

"I did too. We should do it again sometime." The words are out of my mouth before I have a chance to stop them, so I quickly add, "That's if you want to, I mean." Apparently, my heart knows what it wants. My brain isn't doing to do anything to stop us.

"We should do it again. I'll text you."

Fuck yes! I mentally cheer to myself. "Sounds like a plan. I'll see you."

He gives me one last kiss before my phone pings to let me know my ride is here and watches me walk out to the waiting car.

By the time I finally make it to the diner where I'm supposed to meet my father, I'm a solid fifteen minutes late.

Dad sees me walk in and stands, pulling out my chair and kissing my cheek before he takes his seat again. "Rough morning?"

Vice Admiral Rodney Peterson has always been a stickler for being on time, among other things that come with being raised by a man who commands nearly the entire Navy. I'm fully prepared for the lecture about punctuality and know that it's well deserved because this time, that little lecture will be totally worth it.

"You could say that. I, uh, I overslept." Just a tiny white lie. I could have easily fallen asleep in Damon's arms on the deck.

My cheeks flush at the thought.

Laughter rumbles from my Dad's chest. "Right, I'm going to take your word on that and continue to remain blissfully naïve over here...after I ask if this means you've got a date for the charity gala next weekend."

I pinch the bridge of my nose and wince. "Well...not exactly." While the gala has been at the forefront of my mind, finding a date to go with me has not been.

"If you need someone to go with, I'm sure Ryan MacLeod's son would be more than happy to be your plus one. And it would make quite the impression." He grins knowingly.

This gala is important to my father and I know it. Still in his prime, he wants to make a run for Admiral – a highly coveted and prestigious position that includes a lot of politics and showing off. The who's who of DC will be in attendance. It would be mutually beneficial to my job and my dad's if I appeared to be in a relationship. Dating a Senator's son, even for a night, is not on the top of my list of ways to make that happen, though.

"Dad, I know MacLeod is one of your allies, which is all the more reason that I think I really should not mix business with pleasure. God forbid something goes wrong and Ryan's dad decides to use that against you."

Dad takes a sip of his coffee and raises a brow. "Always the smart one. You've got a point. Forget I mentioned it. Anyone else you could bring along?"

Damon comes to mind, and I have to shake my head to clear that thought. Nope. Not happening. Talk about mixing business with pleasure. Taking Damon with me would be the polar opposite end of that scenario. Who's to say he'll actually text me or that we'll even see each other again? He may totally ghost me.

Or he might text me again, and we may spend another night tangled in the sheets and in each other's arms.

"Maeve," Dad clears his throat. "What in the world has got you distracted this morning?"

Oh, if he only knew.

"You know what, Dad, I had a thought." I've got to change the subject entirely.

He eyes me cautiously. "Maeve, why do I feel like you're about to say something crazy?"

"Don't you think it would look good if *you* brought a date to the event? We would look like the perfect little family."

This time he nearly spits out his coffee. "Goddamn. I knew you were up to something."

The look on his face is enough to keep me going, "There's this new dating app. You could try it out. Maybe find you a hot younger woman..."

Dad shakes his head, "Stop. You can stop right there. I won't ask you about your dating life anymore if you promise not to suggest I start dating."

The fit of giggles I've been trying to hold back finally takes over, and I let it all out. "If you could have seen your face. Oh, Daddy. That was priceless."

"Such a smart-aleck. The last thing I need is to get involved in a relationship at my age."

"What did you used to tell me? Love would hit me when I least expected it. Hm. You wait and see, Dad."

"Maeve Louise Peterson, you're not too old for me to take you over my knee."

"Ha. You'd have to catch me first."

Dad snorts. "What am I going to do with you, kid?"

I missed out on so much growing up with my dad constantly deployed. These moments right here tend to make up for it, though. I wouldn't trade it for the world.

NINE
DAMON

Reminders from last night and this morning linger around the place even after Maeve's left. I'm pretty sure I owe Curtis a new lamp for the coffee table, and I should probably consider washing the windows on the patio door. Imprints from Maeve's body have smudged the glass. While I think it would be hysterical to leave something like that behind just to annoy the hell out of my brother, there is an oddly protective part of me that doesn't want to share any piece of Maeve with the rest of the world.

I'm blaming all of these weird feelings floating around in my head on all the mind-blowing sex and endorphins. I mean, come on now, it was one night.

Determined to clear my head, I quickly toss together a protein shake and add some pre-workout powder into the mix, then throw on some gym clothes and head down to the basement of Curtis' townhouse where he's got a full in-home gym set up. Five miles on the treadmill and another two hours lifting weights leave my entire body fatigued. I'm ready for a hot shower and to veg out on the couch for a little bit.

Even completely exhausted, I find it hard to sit around and do nothing. I'm not used to not having chores to do or something to take care of. Only a few minutes after I've landed my freshly showered self on the couch, I'm back up and scrubbing the entire house from top to bottom like a woman hell-bent on nesting. When I'm done, I pick up the phone and call my parents to check in like I usually do every weekend around this time.

My mom picks up on the first ring, and we chat for a while. Dad takes over and askes about the farm and laughs when I tell him that Curtis is in charge for the next two weeks.

"I'm sure he'll do fine. It's you I'm worried about, Son."

"Psh. I'm good."

"Right. I bet your ass hasn't sat down since you got to DC. What the hell are you going to do for two whole weeks?"

I shake my head because they clearly know me all too well. "I'm sure I'll find something. I mean, I'll have to, right?"

"Hell, you better or you'll wind up in trouble, I already know it."

Maeve creeps back into my mind, and I wonder how her breakfast went.

"I could always redecorate Curtis' house for him," I joke, knowing damn well that is possibly the worst idea I could come up with.

My dad chuckles and swears. "Please don't. You remember how pissed he used to get at you when you would go in his room and move things around. You go changing his house, and he's liable to kill you."

Dad's still not wrong, but another idea pops into my head.

"You're already plotting, aren't you, Damon?" Dad asks.

"I am, but it's not what you think." I go on to explain. "I've got a little nest egg going already. I think I might be able to flip this bet with Curtis. Instead of the winner getting $5000, we can throw that money toward an investment property. Build a little more net worth between the two of us. I could look at houses while I'm here and get Curtis down here for a day before I go home to get his thoughts and put in an offer."

"That doesn't sound like a vacation to me. It does sound like a solid idea, though."

My mom chimes in from the background. "Can't you both ever take a break? You must get that from your father."

Mom and Dad may have given up running the family farm and moved to warmer weather, but that doesn't mean Dad stopped working altogether. Instead, he has his own real estate venture going in Florida. I'd be lying if I said he didn't teach me literally everything he knows.

"Runs in the blood. Besides, don't you volunteer at the shelter nearly every day too?" I tease her.

Mom huffs in the background, and Dad and I both laugh at her. "You're a smarty pants, Damon. Idle hands are the devil's playland and all that."

I can imagine her waving me off with one hand on her hip. "So, what was that about a vacation, Ma'am."

"You're not too old for me to whoop you, young man." She threatens, but I know she's smiling on the other end of the line.

"I love you both," I tell them.

"We love you too, Son. We'd better get going. Got somethings to finish up before we head out to dinner with some friends. We'll catch ya later." Dad says.

"Have fun. and you two stay out of trouble."

"Don't make me a grandmother while you're at it. Put a ring on it first," Mom throws in at the last minute.

"Jesus. Goodbye, Mom." I add before hanging up.

A quick glance at the clock tells me that it really is nearly dinner time, and the whole day has passed by. A growl from my stomach reminds me that I managed to skip lunch and need to figure out what I'm eating sooner rather than later. I rummage through the fully stocked kitchen and decide on some chicken and veggies on the grill.

While it cooks, I take the chance to text Maeve.

Me:*Hope breakfast went well.*

We didn't exactly agree on what was happening next, but I know we both said we would be open to getting together again. Maybe this time I can take her on a proper date.

My phone pings with a reply just a few minutes later.

Maeve:*Hey, stranger. I think I may have left my clothes at your place, and I should probably return the ones I borrowed. ;)*

A smile crosses my face.

Me:*Is that your way of asking to see me again?*

I tease and hope that I'm not coming off too pushy.

Maeve:*Would you judge me if I said that's absolutely what I was implying?*

Me: *Hell, no. I'd say we're both on the same page.*

Maeve:*Oh, good! I didn't want to come off as eager.*

Me: *Who text who tonight? LOL.*

Maeve:*Good point. Maybe you're the clingy one, then.*

Me: *You wound me.*

Maeve: *I'm sure you'll survive. Any chance you want to meet up tomorrow?*

Me: *I'll clear my schedule ;)*

Maeve: *Jeez, I'm so lucky. : p*

Me: *You really are. Can I take you to lunch? Maybe a movie?*

Maeve: *Ooo. There's this bistro around the corner from my place that serves the best lunch. I'll text you the address. Meet me there around noon?*

Me: *I'll be there.*

Maeve sends me the bistro's information then excuses herself to finish working on a project while I pull my dinner off the grill and settle down to eat.

Even though this isn't our first date, I feel like I'm in high school all over again and about to take a girl out for the very first time. One thing is for sure, I didn't plan on coming to DC and falling in love – or lust for that matter. I have a feeling my best-laid plans are about to be wrecked.

TEN

MAEVE

"Okay, I gotta hand it to you. I think this is the best chicken Caesar salad and scallop pasta that I've ever had. I totally wouldn't expect that at a bistro." Damon pushes back from the table and pats his stomach.

I try hard not to chuckle because the man still has a six-pack, even though I've just watched him clear an entire plate. Meanwhile, I feel like I'm carrying around a food baby. "We should plan a day to drive up to Baltimore and have some genuine seafood."

"I'm not a complete swine. I've had authentic Maryland seafood before," he sticks his tongue out at me. "That said, I wouldn't be opposed to taking you up on that offer. It has been a while."

"It's settled then. It's going down. Maybe one night after I get off work or sometime next weekend."

"It's a date," he hits me with that damn wink again.

Could it be possible for this man not to make me swoon any harder for him? I'm trying hard to fight off any feelings and live in the moment. He's not helping. Not at all.

"You still want to catch that movie? Apparently, there's a place just outside of town that plays throwback movies. They had some good choices."

I tap my chin. "Hm. I don't know. We could go back to my place and pick something on Netflix."

Damon gives me a flirty look. "Maeve, are you asking me if I want to Netflix and Chill?"

"Maybe? Yes. I'm not sure?" I can feel the heat creeping its way up my neck and into my cheeks.

"You're cute when you get flustered."

This time I toss my napkin at him. "You somehow manage to throw me off-kilter. I'm not sure if I like it or not."

He thinks about that statement for a minute. "I think you like it. Otherwise, we wouldn't be sitting here right now."

I roll my eyes at him. "Whatever you say."

"Come on. I'll take you back to your place, and we can watch a movie on Netflix. I might even keep my hands to myself."

"Something tells me that the probability of you keeping your hands to yourself is slim to none."

"All depends on you, sweetheart."

Having already paid for our meals at the counter, we clean up our table then walk the short distance back to my place.

"This is it," I tell him as I open the door.

Damon steps into the living room and looks around. "It's cozy."

"It's not much, but the apartment serves its purpose for a single gal like me."

The main living area is completely open concept with a kitchen island that serves as a breakfast bar, a living/dining room with a cozy fireplace, a couch, my favorite chaise lounge, and an area where my six-person dining table sits. Along the far wall is a small hallway that leads to the bathroom, bedroom, and laundry room.

The best part is that it's not far from my office, so most days, I walk unless I know I'll be traveling to a venue or to meet with a client.

"It's home. and a heck of a lot more my style than that oversized townhouse Curtis lives in."

"Oh, come on. You have to admit your brother's digs are pretty impressive." I poke his side, which results in him wrapping me up in a bear hug.

"What can I say? I'm a simple man. Next time you come over, though, we'll have to test out the full capacity of that shower of his."

"Mmm. I like the sound of that. Also, I'd like to point out that you're not keeping your hands to yourself."

Damon unwraps me and slides his hands down to my ass for a squeeze before completely letting go. "You're the one who started it by poking my sides."

"Oo. You're ticklish, aren't you?" I go in for the kill again, but he stops me by grabbing my hands and pulling me in close again.

"You promised me a movie first," he says with a kiss to the top of my forehead. "Behave. I'm trying to be a gentleman."

I pout, he chuckles and smacks my ass. "Fine. The remote is on the end table. You pick a movie, I'll grab us some wine. You do drink wine, right?"

"I've been known to savor a glass or two," he says, walking over to the couch and grabbing the remote before getting comfortable.

When I join him on the other end of the sofa, he's got

Love, Guaranteed queued up on Netflix. "Good grief. Really Damon?"

"What?" he feigns innocence.

"Did you read the synopsis?"

He shrugs. "Uh. No. I picked something that looked like a chick flick."

I'm not sure if he's serious or if he's up to something. A movie about a lawyer who falls for a guy who's trying to sue a dating app because they don't hold up to their promise of a happily ever after. That irony is not lost on me. "Okay. Press play then, smarty pants."

Damon hits the button then curls a finger at me. "Come 'ere."

"What happened to hands to yourself?" I smirk.

Damon grabs my feet that are propped up on the couch between us and gives a gentle tug. "I'll make an exception for cuddling. That's it. Nothing wrong with cuddling with a pretty girl and watching a movie, right?"

I give in and move closer so he can put his arm around me, and I can lay on his chest. "I almost wish we would have gone to that movie theater now."

"Yeah. Why's that?" he asks.

"Because then we could make out in the back row like teenagers."

Damon curses, and I smile at the fact that I'm not the only one affected by the chemistry between us. "Baby, if you want to make out like horny teenagers, I'm not going to be the one to say no," he says and tilts my face up to press a kiss to my lips.

What's a girl to do with a response like that? Make out, of course. Why should I not take full advantage of the sexy cowboy sitting right here with me, especially when he's more than willing to please?

By the time the movie ends, I haven't seen a single minute of it. We haven't said two words to each other, and I'm not in the mood for talking. I'm ready to drag Damon to my bedroom and rip all our clothes off.

Until Damon shuts me down.

Bastard.

"Go out with me again. Then, I'll give you what you really want."

I huff. "Isn't that called bribery? Coercion?"

The smug look on his face only serves to wind me up more. "I wouldn't call it that. Think of it as delayed gratification."

"Fine!" I cross my arms over my chest. "You want another date? It's going to have to wait until Tuesday. I've got a full schedule tomorrow and a dinner meeting with a client."

"I'll pick you up from your office at five. Or is that too early for you?"

"I'll be ready at five. I'll text you the office address."

"Don't pout. You can handle waiting a day," he boops my nose then brushes my hair back out of my face.

"Nearly two whole days," I grumble. "Don't worry. I see how you are, Cowboy. Just remember, I can take care of myself."

That comment is enough to stir him up. Damon pushes me onto my back on the sofa and hovers over me. "Take care of yourself all you want while I'm gone. We both know it'll still be my name on your lips when you come."

Holy fuck!

I don't have time to react because he's kissing me breathless again. Let me tell you, I am here for it!

When he stops, I let out an uncontrolled whimper, and he winks. "I'll see you Tuesday."

I want to run after him. To tie him up. Pin him down. Something. Anything. But the asshole has effectively rendered me useless. My entire body feels like it's short-circuited while he simply walks out the door, leaving me like this.

ELEVEN

MAEVE

Waiting until Tuesday to see Damon again sure felt a whole lot like torture. Delayed gratification, my ass. Especially when he made it a point to text me yesterday morning and sent me several texts throughout the day. Then last night, he thought it would be hilarious to start dirty talking to me on the phone. I almost moved around my whole schedule and called off today to see him sooner because it drove me crazy.

I'm still not sold on his whole delayed gratification theory. Even if the anticipation seems more like a sexy game of cat and mouse now that I'm sitting across from him at *The Cheesecake Factory*.

"I hope this is okay. I went with something I knew should be decent." He apologizes as if his choice of restaurants is somehow unacceptable.

"Are you kidding? What could possibly be wrong about amazing food and cheesecake?"

"Good point," he flashes that amazing smile at me, and my breath hitches.

If I'm not careful, I could fall hard for him. That's not part of the plan.

"I don't usually hit up fine dining places back home. Not many around, to be honest." There's a hint of insecurity in his voice.

"It's fun to get dressed up and go out somewhere fancy every once in a while, but I like this much better. Maybe because I spend so much time at upscale events," I explain.

"Events?" he asks.

"Event planner," I explain. The realization that we didn't do a whole lot of talking and don't know a whole lot about each other is not lost on me. "Weddings, some political functions. Galas. All that fun stuff. There's actually a charity gala coming up this weekend. While I'm not 'the' event planner, I did get recruited to be on the committee this year. It's my job to make sure everything is in its place and looks nice."

"No galas back home either. Weddings and funerals mostly," Damon chuckles. "My buddy Gavin got married and was just coming back from his honeymoon right before I left to come here. Had the reception in the old barn on my property."

My eyes light up, and I bounce in my seat. If I had to choose one type of event to do forever, I'm pretty sure weddings would be it. Seeing two people's love story come together forever is one of the biggest honors. "Oh my gosh. I bet it was so romantic. Do you have pictures?" I've only ever been able to do one barn wedding in my whole career, and it was perfect if I do say so myself.

Damon reaches in his back pocket and pulls out his phone. "Darlin', it's nothing like you're used to, I'm sure of it."

He flips the phone around and shows me a few selfies of who I'm assuming are the groomsmen. The guys are all dressed in blue jeans with boots and white dress shirts with khaki vests overtop. Taking the phone from his hand, I flip it sideways to make the image larger. "Oh my God, that's your brother? Holy shit, you two really do look alike."

He lets out a hearty laugh. "That does tend to happen with identical twins. That's Curtis and our buddies, Gavin and Stone. Stone and Gavin are actually cousins, but those three right there, I'd give them the shirt off my back. They're the kind of friends that'll drop everything and show up no matter what time, no questions asked."

"Those kinds of friends don't come along often."

"Ain't that the truth. Our whole little town is a lot like that. Someone needs something, we all pitch in and handle it. It's never about who did what either."

"Is it gossipy, though? I've always thought small towns were the types where everyone knew everything about you."

Damon rubs the back of his neck. "I mean, people talk. It's not usually meant in a mean way. Growing up, if you got in trouble – your parents would know before you even got back to the house. It can't be that much different than rubbing elbows with politicians. There's a whole lot of gossip and mudslinging, right? I'd think you'd see a lot of that here."

I think about it for a minute, "I guess. I try to tune it all out, though." Thoughts of my ex float through my head. Word traveled fast about things with us in our social circle. It's why I've only got a handful of friends that I can trust these days.

He swipes his phone again and shows me a picture of Curtis and a stunning brunette with hair way longer than mine and a kick-ass dress on. "That's Gigi, my brother's fiancé."

"Oh! That reminds me. Totally random and none of my

business, really, but you said your brother's fiancée lived in the townhouse too. Please tell me that you two don't..." I don't get a chance to finish that thought before he interrupts me.

"Nope. She was at my place with Curtis but had to come back home for some reason. Far as I know, she's staying at her apartment now. I actually met her for the first time when they came back home for Gavin's wedding."

"Have you to ever..."

Damon cocks a brow and smirks. "Ever what?"

"You're going to make me say it, aren't you?"

"Oh, I am. I need to hear it."

"Have you ever...dated the same girl?"

"Dated or shared?" he pushes, and I'm pretty sure I want to die of mortification on the spot.

"Forget I asked."

He shakes his head, "We've never dated the same girl or done anything like that. There may have been a drunk dare our senior year where he bet that his girlfriend wouldn't notice if it was him instead of me. It never got that far. She saw my tattoo and immediately knew."

"What about your parents? Did they ever get the two of you confused?" I don't know where this sudden curiosity has come from, but I'm intrigued.

"Not so much. My parents both swear we were like day and night our whole lives. I think most people that know us can tell us apart these days."

I look down at the photo again and really study it for a moment. Damon's right. Even I can see subtle differences between the two of them. Damon's smile lights the whole picture while his brother's doesn't meet his eyes. There's a darkness that seems to linger around him.

"Don't tell me you're crushing on my brother now." Damon teases.

"No! I actually thought that you two *are* distinguishable." I point to the photo, "you're smiling like you're the life of the party, and Curtis seems like he's a lot more serious."

"You could say that." He takes the phone and swipes through a few more photos. "Here's the barn all set up for the wedding. A few of the ranch hands, along with myself and the bridesmaids, put it all together as best we could."

Looking at the photo, I'm blown away at how great it all looks. "First time you ever decorated for a wedding?"

"Yup."

"You sure about that? Doesn't look like something a rookie did." I wink. "It's beautiful."

"Quinn was happy with it. That's what matters."

"Yeah, no one ever wants an unhappy bride."

"She's pretty cool and a good fit for Gavin. He did good." He grins.

"What about you? Ever been in love, engaged? Or wish you were?" I don't know where the brilliant idea came to ask those questions. Too late now.

Damon stutters for a split second until he regains his composure. "Nice little transition there."

"Oh, come on. Don't clam up on me now. I want to know all your dirty secrets."

"Darlin', I don't have secrets. Dirty or otherwise. What you see is what you get."

I playfully kick him under the table. "Well. Out with it then!"

"Fine. Never been engaged. Can't say I've been in love before now. One day, I'd love to have a wife and family of my own," he folds his hands and leans his chin on top of them, watching me intently. "Your turn now."

The way he said he's never been in love before now is not lost on me. Filing it away for later, I ponder my own questions then answer them honestly. "Never engaged. Thought I was in love once. Wished for the white picket fence at one point. I don't exactly trust my heart after that experience."

A conversation that should feel heavy and strained feels completely natural between the two of us. Topics shift naturally, and we talk about daily lives over the rest of dinner. With every single detail we share, I begin to feel closer to Damon than I have with just about anyone else in my life. He's in tune with me. He listens, which makes me feel heard for the first time in a very long time. The way his eyes light up when he talks about his home and family tugs at my heartstrings and makes me crave things I have no business wanting.

When it's time for dessert with both order a slice of cheesecake. Damon goes for classic plain while I decide to indulge in a slice of the turtle cheesecake. The brief silence that follows isn't awkward or tense.

"When do you go back home?" I finally find the courage to ask the question that's been plaguing me all afternoon, after a few bites of the to die for chocolate and caramel mixed with their classic cheesecake.

"In a week, give or take a day or two. Barring that Curtis doesn't need me back sooner."

A twinge of frustration hits me unexpectedly. Of course, he's not staying long. Why would he? His entire lift is in Pennsylvania. This was never meant to be more than a little fling.

"Hey," Damon reaches for my hand and gives it a gentle

squeeze. "You okay? You look like I might have kicked your dog or something."

"What? No. Got caught up in my head for a minute, that's all."

He nods in understanding. "Tend to do that myself from time to time."

"Yeah. So, I told you about my job. I want to hear what a day in your life is like."

Damon smiles and sits up a little straighter. He's proud of his life's work. I admire that.

"It's nothing as fancy as planning galas. Lots of shoveling poop. Making sure all the animals are taken care of. We raise cattle and do some horseback riding lessons. A little boarding too. We've got a little co-op going with the other farmers in our area for crops and stuff. What we don't grow amongst ourselves; we can pick up at the local grocery store. It's a little mom and pop place."

"How small is your town exactly?"

Listening to him go on about the place he grew up in almost sounds like something out of a Hallmark movie. I imagine it's probably one of the cutest little places to visit.

"Do you miss it?"

"I could see myself missing it more if I moved away for good. When I was in the Navy, I couldn't wait to get back home. It's not so bad right now, especially because I've got a pretty lady to keep me company."

"Smooth," I roll my eyes. "Well, Cowboy. Where do we go from here?" I ask once he's paid the bill.

"I was hoping your place or mine." He tells me earnestly. "But if that's not what you want..." his voice trails off.

"I thought you'd never ask."

"Good. I do believe we have some unfinished business

to attend to." Once we're both out of the booth, Damon pulls me into his side and kisses my forehead. "Let's get out of here."

When we end up back at my place, Damon takes over the moment we walk in the door. The mood shifts as heat and sparks build around us. He presses me up against the cool wood and kisses me like I've been dreaming about since he kissed me goodbye Sunday.

I'm lost in the moment with him as he kisses down my neck. His hands trail under the fabric of my shirt and tug it upward until he's cupped my breasts. Damon rolls each nipple between his fingers, pinching and teasing them both into stiff peaks beneath the lace of my bra, and I arch up into his body.

"Fucking beautiful." He numbles against my flesh before sinking to his knees and pulling the heels off my feet.

Damon tugs the black slacks down my legs, making sure to take my panties with him before he drapes my legs over his shoulders and buries his head in my pussy. One swipe of his talented tongue over my flesh has my toes curling and fingers tangled in his hair.

He adds two fingers to the mix. Slipping them inside me, he works his magic, finding the exact spot that forces me to quiver against him. With each movement, I float higher and higher until I can't hold back anymore. The pleasure takes over like a tsunami leaving me completely breathless. I'm calling out his name and begging for all that he can possibly give.

Stars explode behind my eyelids like fireworks. My entire body shakes, and I feel like I'm falling. It's Damon's grip on me that holds me steady through the storm of pleasure. I don't even have a chance to catch my breath before he stands up and swoops me into his arms to carry me to the couch.

"You know, I think that's the most incredible thing I've ever seen," he mumbles against my temple while I bask in post-orgasmic bliss in his lap. "Watching you fall apart. Knowing I'm the one making you that way. I could spend the rest of my life doing that and never get bored."

"Mmm. I bet you say that to all the girls." It's meant to be lighthearted and funny.

When he shifts underneath me and tilts my chin so that I'm starring into two pools of baby blue, I can see the seriousness in his expression. "The only woman I'm talking about is you."

My heart squeezes in my chest. "Oh, Damon." To distract me from the swell of emotions, I work on the buttons on the top of his polo shirt and kiss my way along his jawline before tugging the shirt over the top of his head. "I'm going to have to be careful with you."

"Please don't," he growls as I straddle his waist. "The last damn thing I want you to do is be careful." He pulls my shirt off. I unhook my bra and toss it to the floor behind us.

"Challenge accepted. Prepare to have your world rocked, Cowboy." I raise up off his lap enough that I can get his zipper down and free his hard length. "No boxers? Wishful thinking?"

"Maybe." He lifts up to shove his pants down even further, then guides me right onto his cock with a hiss. "You always feel so good on my cock," he moans with his hands firmly in place on my hips, guiding our movements. "I've missed this."

"Who's the one holding out? Delayed gratification. Isn't that what you called it?" I use his words from Sunday against him, except they're useless when he leans forward takes a nipple into his mouth while he pinches the other in his fingers.

I want to stay right here, consumed by this man and every ounce of pleasure between us. My back arches pushing my chest even further into his face while continuing to rock against him until I forget about everything else around us.

His hips thrust upward, and he pushes me down against him, grinding us together with each movement. Already primed from my earlier orgasm, I can already feel a second one brewing. This one is even more powerful than the first.

"Damon. Oh, God. Yes."

"Goddamn, baby. Come all over my cock." He grunts into the crook of my neck.

"So close." I pant.

"Let go for me. Do it." Damon's command is my undoing.

Falling forward onto his shoulder, I can feel my pussy throbbing and squeezing his cock.

Before the last tremor has left my body, he manages to quickly flip us over and rip his pants off completely. Next thing I know, I'm flat on my back, and he's thrusting into me with all he's got. "So. Damn. Good." He moans with each thrust.

"Fuck, fuck, fuck," his breath hitches, and his pace quickens before he quickly pulls out. Two strokes of his hand, and he's coming all over my stomach. Watching his cock flex with each spurt makes my thighs clench in need. I feel like he's claiming me, marking me as his own.

"Jesus. You're trying to kill me," I manage to sigh.

"You like my cum on you?"

"*That* is the hottest thing I've ever seen."

"I've never done that to anyone before," he admits. "It is pretty fucking hot."

Pushing up onto my elbows, I look him in the eyes. "Hm. I think we should do it again."

Damon doesn't refuse; instead, he rubs his cock in the mess he's already made then slips back inside me for another round.

He's officially ruined me for anyone else. It's too late to stop me from falling. I'm as good as gone when it comes to Damon.

TWELVE

DAMON

Maeve's warm body curls against mine, and she lets out a gentle sigh.

She's content. We both are. Maeve brings me a peace I've never felt before.

"Can I ask you something?" she whispers.

"Yeah, of course."

"What exactly are we doing?"

I look down at her and shake my head. "I'm not really sure what you mean."

"When we matched on Love Bites, it was by mistake. Well, sort of."

I chuckle. "Oooookay." Nothing like being told you were a mistake by the woman you've fucked senseless more than once.

"I was having dinner at the bar. My friend Justin's place. He startled me. I accidently clicked on the button. I hadn't even made up my mind if I was willing to put myself out there again."

That makes me feel remotely better. At least Maeve isn't saying *we* are an accident. "I ain't going to offend you if

I tell you that I was drunk when I signed up for the app, am I?"

Maeve covers her mouth and giggles. "You're lying."

"Never told a lie. I drank six beers, something I rarely do. Suddenly I thought I'd need something to do for the next two weeks. The next thing I know, I see this ad on social media for this app. I remember it said something about for those looking for forever and those looking to have a little fun. I thought the fun part sounded like a good plan."

"That's all I wanted was a little fun."

"Is that right?" I twirl a strand of her light brown hair around my finger. "and how'd that work out for you?"

Maeve sits up and straddles my waist. "I'd say it worked out really well. I mean, I thought we'd be one and done, but if it were up to me, I'd spend the next however many days we've got with you. Right here. I think that may just be enough fun to last me a lifetime."

"I'm not sure if I should be offended or flattered, but with your sweet little cunt rubbing on me like that, I can't be bothered to care."

"Oh, it's a compliment," she leans forward and pins my hands over my head before she kisses me. "Now, you hold tight, Cowboy. It's my turn."

What is it about this woman that makes me lose control? I'd never let anyone else pin me down and do the things she's doing to me right now. It's something about watching Maeve take over that is better than I could ever imagine. I'll gladly let this woman have her wicked way with me any day, any time.

Maeve has her fun, using my body for her pleasure and torturing me along the way. When she's done, I flip us both over and bury myself inside her wet heat. With my thumb circling her clit, she gives way to the second round of pleasure. Calling out my name and digging her heels into my back.

Thoughts from earlier in the evening, blowing my load all over her stomach, play through my mind over and over again until my cock starts throbbing insider her.

This time when I collapse beside her, she pulls the sheet over both of us and yawns. My eyelids feel heavy, and I've got no choice but to give in to sleep. Until we're both woken up by her alarm clock at six o'clock. She grumbles and stretches her naked body against me.

"Morning," I grumble back.

"Hm. What I wouldn't give to call out and spend all day right here." She purrs, using her delicate hands to rub all over my body.

I'm already on board. The brain between my legs is standing at attention.

"Aren't you, the boss?"

"Yes, yes, I am. Which means I've got way too many things to handle today. That includes meeting with the planning committee for the charity event I told you about at dinner last night."

"I bet you look sexy as hell when you're in the zone and doing your thing." I muse out loud. I can't help but wonder if she wears one of those hot little power suit numbers with fuck-me heels when she's meeting with clients.

"Oh, it's so sexy," she snorts and sits up, leaving me disappointed and craving more. "I'm going to go get ready. You can go back to sleep until I leave if you want."

She's not rushing me out the door, and I'm damn sure not in any hurry to leave. An interesting situation for two people who set were only looking for a little fun.

Before she escapes me completely, I pull her back to me and give her a kiss. "There ain't go going back to sleep. How about I make us some coffee? Please tell me you own a coffee pot." If not, I'm damn sure going to have to find someplace nearby for caffeine.

"I do. Everything is easy to find in the kitchen. Coffee mugs are in the cabinet over the top of the coffee pot. I like mine with cream and sugar."

"You got it. I'll leave you to it because if I have to watch you get ready, you'll never make it out the door."

"Very tempting," she contemplates as she shimmies her way into the bathroom.

Keeping my promise, I slip my boxers and jeans on then pad through her apartment to the kitchen.

Once the coffee is brewing, I take a look in the fridge and pull out some eggs. Making myself right at home, I locate a frying pan then cook up two eggs with a side of toast for both of us. When the coffee is done brewing, I pour two mugs full and add cream and sugar to hers, hoping I got it right.

"Oh my God, you cooked me breakfast," Maeve gasps as she stumbles into the kitchen, fully dressed but with her hair still wrapped in a towel. "You do know, this isn't usually how this is supposed to work, right? You don't have to cook breakfast or even make me coffee."

"Hey, I can take it all back if you want."

Maeve pulls her plate even closer and points her fork at me. "Don't you dare."

I raise my hands, "All right, I won't take your food."

"You can't have my coffee back either," she narrows her eyes at me in a warning.

"Oh, heaven forbid I take the coffee."

"Never the coffee." She smirks. Maeve takes a few bites then looks up at me. "You know, Damon. I think I like you a little bit."

"Really? Hm. I guess I like you a little bit too."

"I mean it. I feel pretty stupid saying this but, I felt it the night we met. I can't put my finger on it, and I don't know what to make of it. It's just different."

"I've heard people say it happens like that sometimes. Never thought anything of it until you."

She pauses for a beat. "What are you saying?"

"I'm saying, I like you too. It's pretty clear that we've got some chemistry, and sure, there's be a whole lot of sex, but even without that...the moments when we manage to keep our hands off each other...there is substance there." I leave off the fact that we're from two different worlds and live a couple hours apart.

Why couldn't I have met Maeve in my hometown?

"I meant what I said last night about doing this. Whatever this is."

"So, not a mistake then?" I can't help but give her a hard time on that one.

"No. Certainly not a mistake, or at least the best mistake I ever made."

Ain't that the truth. Leaving town in a few days is going to sting like hell.

"Then I guess you're stuck with me for a little while," I tell her with a smile.

We both finish eating then Maeve dashes off to fix her hair while I clean up the dishes and pull on the shirt from last night and my boots. Doesn't take long before she's back and ready to go.

"So, when will I see you again?"

She sighs, "I went and said all that, but I'm swamped the rest of the week. The gala is this weekend, and there's a whole lot to take care of." Maeve hesitates, "Although, dare I ask...would you want to be my plus one at the gala this weekend? Don't feel like you have to say yes. You are the one who said you'd love to see me in my element, though."

I don't need to think twice, "Sure. I'll be your plus one. Just tell me what I need to do."

"Hm. Dress to impress. Suit and tie. Be yourself. That's all."

"I think I can manage." I'm sure Curtis has a suit I can borrow. If not, there's got to be rental places around.

"Great!" she pats my cheek. "I'm looking forward to seeing you all dressed up."

"I bet you are," I reply with an added eyebrow waggle for good measure.

Maeve rolls her eyes, "Okay, I really need to get going. I'll call you later?" she asks as I follow her out the door and wait for her to lock up.

We step on the elevator hand in hand. "What about meeting up for lunch? I know you said you were busy this week, but you've still got to eat. I'll come to you."

"I can always use a little midday break. I'll text you the address to my office. Meet me there at 12:30?"

The elevator doors open in the lobby, and we head for the front exit. "I'll see you at 12:30 then. Anything in particular you like?"

"Anything is fine, really. I appreciate it." Maeve hits me with a breathtaking smile then plants a kiss on my lips. "I'll see you then."

THIRTEEN
MAEVE

It's a good thing that after leaving Damen this morning, I find myself filled with a renewed sense of purpose and inspiration. Despite lack of sleep, I'm energized and ready to take on the day. Floating on cloud nine, especially since he agreed to come with me to the gala, even if I shocked myself when the invitation slipped out of my mouth. So much for avoiding that idea. He keeps me off-kilter and has me wanting and feeling things I have no business even thinking about.

With the gala less than four days away, my list of to-dos seems to keep growing on me, so I can't stop and analyze anything between us.

The first thing on my schedule is a quick meeting with the event manager at *The Washington House,* where the gala is taking place. I need to check in to make sure all of the decorations have arrived and they're set up with everything they need to begin setting up Friday. The ten-minute drive to the venue from my place is made that much better with the warm cup of coffee that Damon sent me out the door with.

After talking with the manager, I'm assured that everything is in place. I feel confident that everything has been taken care of. We both agree that I'll stop back by Friday night to double-check the set up one last time before Saturday.

Thanks to traffic, I make it to the office just in time for my ten o'clock video meeting with the rest of the planning committee. We all review everything on our respective lists, effectively keeping each other in the loop about where we're at. I'm relieved to hear that the caterer who jumped on at the last minute has fulfilled every request and is ready for a flawless setup and serving of food. The committee member in charge of event tickets lets us know that we have sold all 5,000 tickets that we had available and that we've gotten some generous donations from popular local names like our sports teams, as well as a few big names in Hollywood. With the cost of the tickets and the lineup of auction items, there's a good chance that we could exceed our goal for this Gala.

Excitement bubbles, and I find myself truly looking forward to this event even more now. Knowing that I'm playing a crucial part in providing shelter for families in need is humbling.

After meeting with the planning committee, I log in and check my emails for the first time today.

As usual, my inbox is overflowing with new client requests and follow-up information from clients I'm currently working with. I notice the request from Congressman Nolan's wife at the top of my pile. When I click on her email, I'm excited to see that she's finally narrowed down a few days in which she wants to host her luncheon as well as her preference for locations. The list that she's given me is short and sweet. This shouldn't be hard to take care of. So, I hop on the phone and call her first choice for location to see if they have availability. It looks like we're both in luck because District Gardens has an opening on the first available date that Mrs. Nolan is interested in.

I quickly book the venue then email Mrs. Nolan back with the information and an invoice for the deposit.

With that item crossed off my list for the day, I move on to the next email. Before I know it, my stomach is growling, and it's nearly lunchtime.

There's a knock on my office door. I smile to myself, thinking that it's probably Damon waiting on the other side. When the door opens, I'm greeted by my father instead. I take a quick look at the clock on my computer and realize that it's only a little after twelve in the afternoon. That's when I notice the reminder that my assistant added to my calendar too about lunch with my father today.

Whoops.

"Oh my gosh, Dad, you're early," I laugh, not surprised that he's here fifteen minutes before our scheduled lunch date. "You're totally not going to believe this," I start to tell him.

"What's up? Tell me you didn't forget about your old man, did you?"

"Well, kind of." I shrug and bat my lashes at him like I used to do when I was a little girl and was trying to stay out of trouble. "and I may or may not have made plans with someone else for lunch."

Right on cue, my assistant buzzes me on the intercom. "Hey, Maeve. There's a gentleman named Damon here to see you.

"and that would be him," I tell my dad and then let my assistant know that she can go ahead and send Damon.

It's probably not cool of me to throw him straight into the lion's den, but I don't have a choice either way. At this point, their paths are going to cross. Might as well pull the Band-Aid off and get this done and over with

Dad laughs and shakes his head, "Oh, so this is a gentleman caller, huh?

"Don't you start!" I say with an eye-roll, "But yes, he did agree to come with me to the gala, so there's that. Please be nice to him, Daddy."

Damon walks into my office and freezes when he sees there's someone else here too. "Oh, I'm sorry your secretary said I could come on back. I didn't realize you were with someone." He starts to back up, "I can wait out here or come back."

"Damon, meet my father."

For a brief moment, Damon looks slightly intimidated. I have to do my best not to laugh at him. I guess to most people, my dad appears to be a little intimidating, but he's just my father, and I've always been Daddy's Little Girl. That means I know how to get my way and turn him into a big pile of mush. In my eyes, he's always been nothing more than a big teddy bear.

"Damon. I'm Rodney Peterson. It's nice to meet you, son." My dad holds out his hand.

Damon quickly sets the bags down on one of my office chairs and shakes my father's hand, "Damon Knightley. It's nice to meet you, Sir. I apologize; I had no idea that you would be here. Maeve and I were going to have lunch together, but the good news is I did bring extra if you want to join us."

I'm not sure whether to be shocked at Damon's invitation for my dad to stay for lunch or flattered. To be honest,

I'm interested to see what my dad will do next. Will he stay for lunch and subject Damon to the Peterson Interrogation, or will he politely decline if leaving the two of us alone?

"I appreciate the offer. I think just because it will embarrass my favorite daughter, I'm going to take you up on it. Especially since Maeve forgot about lunch with dear old dad, and I'm assuming you have something to do with that."

Damon hesitates for just a second and then chuckles, "I'm really sorry about that. I promise it wasn't my fault, though."

"Oh, he is totally lying! It's totally his fault. I would have never forgotten such a thing had he not asked me to go to lunch with him," I joke with both of them.

Not missing a beat, Damon defends himself, "Hey, you said you had a hectic week at work. I was just trying to make sure you were taking care of yourself and that you ate lunch. It is not my fault you didn't consult your calendar first."

My dad looks at me, and his eyes twinkle with mischief, "You know what, Maeve, I think I like this one."

I think I like this one too and that right there is the problem.

"Well, if you two agree to play nice, let's get on with it. I do have to get back to work eventually." I warn them both.

I clean off the small conference table in the corner of my office and wipe it down. Damon takes out some paper plates and sets them on the table along with the Chinese food that he ordered. He wasn't lying when he said he ordered more than enough food.

While we're eating, Dad has no problem questioning Damon, who is taking it all in stride. Usually, I would actually put my phone down and eat, especially with company. Since they're both so busy chatting with each other that they damn near ignore me, I use the chance to finish up with a few emails.

That is until my ears perk up when they get on the topic of the Navy, and Damon mentions to my dad that he served four years straight out of high school. Dad may be pretty chill with me, but I'm slightly concerned that my dad will look down on Damon for this, mainly since my dad chose a career in the Navy and at the level he did, too.

Dad asks him something about what ship he was on. That's when Damon learns that he's eating lunch with a Vice Admiral. There's trepidation in Damon's eyes, but he takes his cue from my dad, who surprises me by acting like it's no big deal. Instead, he commends Damon for chasing his own dreams and tells him that he respects and appreciates the time he did serve.

Seeing them get along so well is only going to make our goodbye harder.

All too soon, my half-hour lunch break flies by. The guys kindly clean up after us then my dad says his goodbyes with a kiss on my cheek and a shake of Damon's hand.

"I'll see you at the gala on Saturday," he says to both of us.

"We'll be there," I tell him as he steps out of my office and closes the door behind him.

"Maeve, Maeve, Maeve. Did you set me up?" Damon stalks toward me and eyes me suspiciously.

His close proximity heats my entire body. "N...no. I honestly forgot my dad was coming for lunch today."

"Tsk, tsk, tsk." He kisses my neck.

"Uhuh. No, you do not. Don't you dare distract me. I really have to get back to work." I try to put space between us because if I'm not careful, I have a feeling I'll be sprawled out across my desk. That idea is all too appealing. Being even further behind is not.

"I'll let you go. For now. I'll see you tonight?" he resigns.

"It might be late. I'll message you when I finish up." I promise.

"Fair enough," he kisses my forehead. "Later."

Mixed emotions roll through my head for the first part of the afternoon until I become so caught up in the rest of my tasks at hand that all thoughts of Damon and my father's interactions have completely slipped my mind.

It's well after six when I finally finish up for the day, and it doesn't take long for the earlier confusion over my heart, and my mind comes flooding back.

I thought we both went into this with clear expectations. It damn sure didn't take long for those expectations to go out the window and feelings to get involved. Who would have ever thought that I would start to fall in love with someone after a whopping five days?

Love. Damnit. No. I can't love him.

Our relationship or whatever you want to call this has an end date. There is no room for love.

Scared that I'm already in too deep with someone who has the potential to hurt me by walking away, I tell myself it may be wise to put a little space between Damon and me tonight.

I dial his number, fully prepared to let him know that I'm exhausted, and that I should just head back to my place and get some rest. When his voice comes on the line, I can't seem to find the words.

"There you are. I was about to call you and check-in. You said you would be working late, so I made dinner. It's still warm. I can bring it to you unless you want to come here."

"I guess I'm coming over for dinner then."

Damon's thoughtfulness and the need to care for me seems to extend well beyond the bedroom. Yet, one more reason why this thing between us is so dangerous. There's no way I can deny him.

FOURTEEN
DAMON

After a relaxing evening with Maeve the night before, you would think that I'd be a lot more tolerant of this jackass that I'm currently dealing with. I can't believe Zeke referred me to this guy.

"As you can see, this one has been completely remodeled and is move-in ready. I added it to our list since it was in such close proximity to the other properties you wanted to look at," the real estate agent explains. "Two bedrooms, one bathroom, sixteen hundred square feet. Attached garage."

"and you said the unit next door was also available?"

"It's due to be listed by the end of the week. The listing agent said they're finishing up a few more things."

"Hm. The price is a little more than I'm looking to spend." I tell him.

I also told Greg on the phone that I was explicitly looking for fixer-uppers. I don't get why this guy is so hard-pressed to sell me something move-in ready for an investment property. That wasn't the plan Curtis and I agreed on.

"I think you'll find the market value on it is pretty

comparable to the location."

"You do know that I'm not looking to move into this place myself? Like I said, I'm looking for something that I can put some sweat equity into and either sell or rent for a profit. I don't want something that's going to saddle me with a fifteen or thirty-year mortgage."

"I'm not sure you're going to find anything that you're going to be able to pay cash for."

Something about the way the words come out of Greg's mouth pisses me off. Hell, to be honest, Greg has been pissing me off since we got to the very first property today. I'm used to people underestimating or misjudging me, but I don't deal with assholes who think they know what's best for me when it comes to business.

"One, I didn't say anything about paying cash for the entire property. Two, let's be honest here, I don't think you even reviewed the pre-qualification letter that I came to the table with. I gave you a list of properties that I was interested in. We've seen two of those ten."

"Mr. Knightly, I do understand where you're coming from, and I have no doubts about what you can afford. I simply think that you may be confused about the current housing market here in DC."

"You know what, buddy, I think I'm going to go ahead and pass on this property and maybe keep considering my options. How about I give you a call if I decide I want to look at anything else?" I tell Greg. He doesn't need to know that I won't be calling him back when I decide which property I want to look at next.

I DON'T KNOW why I assumed that looking for real estate property in Washington DC would be easy with

Greg, who's acted like an uptight prick since we met. It's kind of funny how some people around here seem to think that just because I wear faded Wranglers and cowboy boots, I must be some kind of dumbass and that I'm dirt poor.

IT DOESN'T REALLY MATTER what they think anyway. Now that my brother is on board with this idea and excited to invest in some property with me, I'm even more hopeful about how things may work out. Plus, investing in properties around the DC area gives me the perfect excuse to come back and visit with Maeve.

Speaking of Maeve, I can't seem to keep her off my mind. Taking her lunch wasn't enough. I had to go and cook her dinner last night, too. I even tried to bring her lunch again today, but she shot me down because she was having a work lunch with her employees.

Last night she mentioned being exhausted. I guess I have myself to blame for that one. Still, I'm hoping that I'll be able to convince her to grab some dinner or a few drinks with me after work tonight since I seem to crave being around her.

The first thing that I need to do before I worry about tonight is get out of this house and as far away from Greg as I can before I say or do something stupid and unprofessional.

Greg finally nods in agreement with my last statement and takes the hint. I go ahead and see myself out, getting into my car and heading back to the townhouse to regroup and figure out if I can find a different real estate agent to help us view some properties.

The minute I walk into the door at Curtis's, my cell phone rings.

Speaking of the devil. My brother's number flashes on the screen.

"Curtis, what's up?" I answer.

"Uhm. Well, I've got some bad news."

"What the fuck did you do to my farm?" I snap. Maybe I'm really the one who needs to get some sleep.

"I didn't do anything, but one of the horses is pretty sick. Gavin said it looks like it might be the flu."

"Son of a bitch. That's nothing you could have done," I begin to apologize for snapping at him.

"Oh, I'm well aware," Curtis replies.

"Where's Gavin?"

"With the vet right now. He told me to get on the phone and call you."

"Let me grab my stuff, and I'll be on my way. Goddamn it. Fuck. Which horse is it?"

"It's Sandi."

Damnit. Sandi's mine. Had her since I was sixteen. The flu in horses is nothing to mess with. "Tell Gavin to call me as soon as he's done with the vet."

I toss my phone on the counter and curse. Depending on how soon they caught it, this could go south real goddamn quick. If I hurry, I can get back to the farm before dark to see what's going on for myself.

Most of the things I brought with me are things I can live without until I come back, so I only take time gathering what I need to take home with me and making sure everything is turned off or locked up. Once I've got it all together, I grab my keys and phone off the counter and head right back out the door to my truck. Fifteen minutes later, I'm gassed up, heading north on the highway, and waiting for Gavin to give me a call.

FIFTEEN
MAEVE

This week's staff meeting is taking place at *Sit & Sip*. After running full steam ahead this week with everything we've got going on, I felt like my employees deserved a bit of a break and a few drinks on me.

Before our food arrives, I raise my glass and begin to speak, "I wanted to take a moment before we get started to thank all of you for your hard work. Those of you that have stepped up and volunteered extra time working with me on the finishing touches for tomorrow's gala, as well as those of you who have been working your respective events this week as well. I've gotten a lot of really positive feedback from the clients. They couldn't be happier with the service we've provided them. I'm really proud to have you on my team. And of course, to Victoria, the world's best assistant. I'd be lost without you, girl. Now, everyone enjoy the afternoon, and I'll see y'all at the gala tomorrow night."

All ten of the employees sitting in front of me smile appreciatively and raise their glasses to cheer. Yes, I was the gracious employer who purchased tickets for everyone who works for me and a plus one because they all deserve a whole lot of recognition and rewards for doing all that they do. It's because of them that I could even begin to fathom affording such a gift for them, and I don't take that for granted.

"Enough with the sappy stuff now. Feel like crying into my apple juice," Victoria tips her glass at me and rubs her pregnant belly. I swear the woman reminds me of Penelope from *Criminal Minds* with her since of style and ever-changing hair.

"I really hope that baby stays in your belly for a full forty-weeks."

"Maeve, I really hope that when you finally settle down and get knocked up that you're just as miserable as I am, you bitch." Victoria laughs at me. "Hello, twenty-six weeks, and I still have occasional bouts of morning sickness."

"Okay, that was purely selfish on my part. I'm sorry," I apologize and give her a hug. "I just don't know what I'm going to do without you until you come back to work."

"Girl, you and I both know you'll do fine. You managed before me; you'll manage without me."

"Uhm, that doesn't mean I want to manage anything without you, duh."

"Oh, hey! Look who it is! Justin said you would be in this afternoon," Marcie walks up and joins us.

"Oh my God, you're home for a change." I drape one arm over her shoulder. "I've missed your face."

"What's this rumor I heard about you and a dating app?" Marcie immediately goes in for the kill.

Victoria's face lights up, and she leans her elbows on the table to set her face on top of her hands like a little kid. "Ooooo, girl. He is f-i-n-e with a capital F. He came by the office yesterday and had lunch with her...and Rodney."

Leave it to my assistant to spill all the tea.

"Shut up. Did he? Sounds serious," Marcie wags her eyebrows at me.

"Whatever, it wasn't planned. It was more like a scheduling conflict." I try to play it off.

"Tell her how they hit it off, though, and how he's coming with you Saturday night!" Victoria squeals like a schoolgirl.

"Remember how I said you were the best assistant ever? I take it back."

Victoria is not phased at all. "Oh, wait a minute," she quickly digs through her purse and pulls out her phone. "I might have taken a picture of him when he came in."

Sure enough, Victoria is not lying. My assistant really did take a picture of Damon, or a picture of one of his best assets, actually.

Marcie cracks up, "You took a picture of his ass."

"That is a good picture, though. Wait. Why did you take a picture of my...I... Damon's ass?"

"You were getting ready to call him yours. Oooo, look at you. Staking your claim and everything." Marcie goads.

"I hate all of you. I was not about to claim him."

"She was totally about to claim him," Victoria chimes in.

"Does the rest of him look that good too?" Marcie asks.

"Heard that!" Justin calls out from behind the bar resulting in Marcie flipping him the finger.

"I'm married. Not dead. You know whose bed I'm sleeping in."

"I'm not going to answer you," I tell Marcie, knowing damn well that I'll be texting her a picture of Damon later when Victoria isn't around to give me hell about it.

"Is he coming by tonight? You're going to hang around for a bit, right?" she asks.

"I'm not sure what he's up to, actually." Realizing that

it's been a few hours since I heard from him, I check my phone only to find no new messages or missed calls.

"Well, let's hope that he stops by. I want to meet him. I'll let you get back to your employees, for now, we'll catch up later," Marcie says before she wanders off into the kitchen area.

The closer it gets to quitting time, the more people filter into the bar, and one by one, my employees start to head home to their families until it's just me left. I recheck my phone. Nothing new from Damon

Rather than sit around all night trying to analyze if or why he's avoiding me, maybe I should call him. He may be caught up in something and forgot to call.

When Justin comes back to check on me, I let him know that I'm going to step outside to make a phone call and then slip out the bar's side door. Damon's phone rings six times, then clicks over to voicemail. I hang up without leaving a message. He'll either call back or he won't. It's not the first time that I've suddenly been stood up by a guy.

SIXTEEN

DAMON

"Hey, pretty girl. You couldn't think of a better way to get me to come back home?" I rub Sandi's cheek.

Her stall was my very first stop as soon as I pulled in the driveway.

"Keaton said she was already pretty dehydrated. It came on quick." Gavin's voice startles me.

When I look over my shoulder, my best friend is propped up against the door frame with his arms over his chest, watching me.

"Usually does. We both know that."

He nods. "Bentley is symptomatic now, too," Gavin delivers the next strand of bad news. "I'm sorry."

"Great. Christ, I hope they all don't catch it." Equine flu travels fast, so it's possible that every horse in this stable could have it.

"I'm sorry. One minute everything was fine. The next minute Sandi was acting weird. I called Keaton as soon as I noticed."

"Ain't nothing you could have done about it." I remind him.

"I'm glad that we built that barn for boarding and didn't have anyone else's horses in here."

"Ain't that the damn truth. Talk about a small miracle."

Exhaustion is written all over Gavin's face. I know he's likely worried himself to the bone today too.

"It's late. You should get on home to your wife. I'm sure she's waiting on you," I tell him.

"Not a chance in hell. If I leave, you're going to sit out here all night with Sandi."

"Gavin, I'm going to sit out here with her no matter what. Ain't no sense in both of us being up all damn night. One of us should get some sleep. Still got a farm to run come sunrise."

"That's cute. You think I'm going to be able to sleep. Someone's got to keep an eye on Bentley, too. So, fuck right off."

"Curtis can watch Bentley." I push back.

"Curtis *is* watching Bentley," my brother says as he walks in the barn. "He's holding steady at the moment. Came over here to check on you and bring you some food since I'm willing to bet you didn't bother to eat dinner."

"Listen, I know the two of you cannot possibly have missed me that much. Did you screw something else up? What aren't you telling me? Why are you both being so nice to me?" I halfheartedly taunt them.

"I think two sick horses is enough. I owe you five grand for that." Curtis shakes his head in disbelief, then looks at my horse, "Way to lose the bet for me, Sandi."

Gavin snorts, "You didn't tell me five-grand was on the line."

"Wasn't sure whose side you would take. I was going to spend that money on fixing up the old' Harley." I tell him.

"Wash up and eat. She'll be alright for five minutes

while you inhale some food," Curtis kicks my foot. "It's still warm. Stone's momma sent it over."

"You and Stone been hanging out?" I ask while heading to the feed room to wash up my hands.

"Something like that," Curtis mumbles. "We don't need to talk about me. What the hell have you been getting into while you've been gone?"

Maeve crosses my mind. "Fuck." I pat my pockets in search of my phone. Shit. Where the hell did I leave my phone? "I'll be right back. I need to go check the truck for something."

I find it still in the vent clip holder with one missed call from Maeve. *Damnit*. It's midnight. She's probably already in bed. It's too late to call her back now.

"Find what you were looking for?" Gavin asks when I walk back into the barn.

"Yeah. Left my phone," I wave it in the air, then slip it in my pocket.

Curtis asks if was expecting a call and the good-natured ribbing starts all over again.

I try to play it cool. "Who says I was waiting on a call? I wanted to make sure I had my phone in case of an emergency."

Gavin so graciously reminds us all that there's a land-line not even ten feet away in the barn office.

"Y'all stop picking on me. I'm worried about my pony." I pull the pity card.

"That's rich. Not even ten minutes ago, you were playing all tough guy and shit." Gavin rolls his eyes.

"He met someone," Curtis says matter of factly.

"How would you know?" I challenge.

That same cocky smile that stares back at me in the

mirror every morning spreads across my twin's face. "You really want to know how I know?"

"I want to know," Gavin answers for me.

Curtis gives me another chance to figure it out, "think about it, Day."

How would he know that I met someone? Unless he had someone spying on me. I freeze. *He wouldn't.*

"Ohhh, it's starting to click, isn't it?" He taunts. "You owe me a lamp."

Motherfucker. "You son of bitch." I drop the plate of food I was about to eat and start to go after him.

Gavin steps between us and slaps me upside the head. "Chill out, so you don't stress your horse out."

"You're so fucking lucky right now," I grumble and cut my eyes at him.

"Don't worry, that was the only part I saw. I turned the cameras off after that. Scared for life."

Gavin nearly loses his mind laughing at my expense. "You recorded him?"

"It wasn't like that. It started recording when dipshit forgot to turn it off at three in the morning."

"Christ. You better have deleted all of it."

"Was she hot?" Gavin asks.

"Gavin. Do not make me fuck you up. I will whip both your asses."

They both flip me off.

"She's smokin' hot," I add with a smirk. "That's all I'm telling either of you."

They don't need to know that I may damn well be falling head over heels for a woman I've only known for a few days. Never believed in love at first sight, but Maeve may make a believer out of me.

Sandi whimpers, diverting my attention. "What is it, girl? Do you want to try to eat?"

"I'll make her some warm food. Keaton said it might help." Gavin volunteers.

When he walks away, Curtis assures me that he really did delete it all and only saw the lamp incident. All I can do at this point is shrug. I shouldn't be surprised, considering he's the guy who made a career out of cybersecurity and tech.

After we try to get Sandi to eat, Curtis and Gavin take turns sleeping on the cot in the office while the other keeps me company. They try to get me to get some rest too, but I'm not going to. Not when Sandi whimpers whenever I leave her side.

Instead, I remain vigil throughout the night.

Darkness eventually gives way to the sunrise. Animals start waking up, and the farm comes to life. Ranch hands and the rest of the staff start buzzing around, getting ready to work for the day. The energy is contagious. Only been gone a week, back for less than twenty-four hours, and realizing just how much I really missed this place.

Can a man really have his heart in two places?

Gavin and Curtis check on all the other horses. Keaton strolls in to check on Sandi and Bentley.

"Got up a little early and figured I'd stop by here before I get started with my regular schedule," Keaton holds out a cup of coffee. "Thought you might need this."

"Thanks, I appreciate the coffee and the early morning house call."

Keaton grew up with me and Curtis. Graduated the same year. We went into the military while he headed off to veterinary school. Took over his dad's practice after earning his degree, and he's been our vet ever since. Like everyone else in this town, we tend to look out for each other.

"How'd she do last night?"

"Didn't really eat. Drank a little bit. Whined a lot like she's in pain. Doesn't seem any worse," I fill him in.

"The fact that she's not getting worse is a plus," he says while looking her over.

He's nearly finished with her exam when Gavin comes back in. The look on his face tells me he's got more bad news. "Hey, Keaton. We've got two more showing symptoms." He comes right on out with it.

"Fuck." I hiss. "Who?"

"Sable and Snowball," Gavin tells me. "I can stay with Sandi if you want to go see for yourself."

Keaton speaks up. "I think Sandi is stable enough that she doesn't need a babysitter, guys. She's not any worse. In fact, I'd venture to say that she may be a smidge better." He cleans off all of his supplies and puts them back in his bag. "We can go take a look at the others together."

I rub Sandi's cheek one more time and tell her to stay out of trouble, then follow the guys to the outdoor stalls where the rest of the horses are separated.

Keaton does exams while I make my rounds and check on all our horses. I hope like hell that Sable and Snowball are the last two that caught this bug and that we've caught it early enough to treat it. Every animal on this farm serves a purpose and is a part of our team. I can't afford to lose four horses, emotionally or otherwise.

SEVENTEEN

MAEVE

I pull up outside The Washington House, letting out a deep breath before getting out of the car and handing my keys off to the valet. The rest of the planning committee has just arrived too. We've got two hours before guests start coming to make sure everything is set up and ready to go.

I locate the events manager and check in with him. He takes us all on a final walk through the ballroom where volunteers and staff are putting the final touches on auction items' displays. Guest tables are already set to perfection. The mini-stage is set up, and the DJ is setting his equipment up. A handful of volunteers are setting up the red carpet in the hallway and the backdrop for pictures. The photographer will be here soon. The catering staff is ready to go and prepping all the dinner selections. Everything has fallen into place after months of planning and preparation. And I've got no one to share the excitement with.

I was able to distract myself yesterday with work and most of today with getting ready for tonight. Now that I'm here, it's hard to ignore the thousand and one thoughts running through my mind.

Damon promised he would show up. But I haven't heard from him since Thursday morning so now I have my doubts. I never really thought I was insecure before. Now there's a part of me that wonders what could have happened and if this is a sign that we're already over.

"Maeve," one of the other committee members, Rebecca, taps my arm to get my attention.

"Sorry. Whatcha need?"

"Mr. Sloan is here and wanted to meet with us before everyone starts arriving," she explains.

"Oh. Okay. Great." I follow her out into the hallway where the CEO of *No More Sleepless Nights* is waiting.

He takes a few minutes to thank all of us for dedicating the time and energy to making tonight happen and shares some of the preliminary numbers with us. Not only did the event sell out, but they set up an online auction for the items that were donated as well. The night hasn't even begun, and we're already several thousand dollars over our first goal for the event.

"These things don't come together without a stellar team. I think it's also imperative to acknowledge Maeve Peterson with Peterson Events and Marketing. Maeve was a newcomer to this side of the event this year, and I have to say that I think I speak for all of us when I say that she blew us away with her talent and attention to detail. I'd like to take this opportunity to formally extend the offer to you and your company a spot as the official event planner for all of our events. We can work out details later, but *No More Sleepless Nights* would love to have you on our team."

Tears threaten to fall from my eyes as I look around at the entire team that helped put it all together. Everyone is looking at me with smiles on their face and applauding. This is a tremendous honor and responsibility. I think I'm in shock. It's a pivotal moment in my career, a moment I've been waiting for.

"and with that, I want to thank everyone one more time for all your hard work. Now, I'm being told that guests are beginning to arrive so, let's get this party started." Mr. Sloan concludes.

Everyone shakes my hand, both thanking and congratulating me as we disburse. I excuse myself and find the closest restroom to take a quick breather and pull myself together. I'm a mixed ball of emotions over everything right now, and I'd be lying if I said I wasn't missing Damon too. How the hell did some boy from a small town walk right in and pull down all the walls I thought I'd built around my heart?

With one more deep breath and a dab of powder on my face, I force myself out of the restroom to greet guests and make my rounds.

The tiniest hint of relief sweeps over me when I see my dad's smiling face in the hallway. "Ah, there's my little girl," he pulls me in for a hug and kisses my forehead. "You look beautiful, young lady. And I heard from Mr. Sloan himself that he's been blown away by the work you've put into this event. I'm so proud of you."

"Thanks, Daddy. That means a lot."

"Where's Damon? I haven't seen him."

The façade I tried to put on feels like it's going to slip away into a puddle of tears at my feet. "I'm afraid he's not coming. I haven't heard from him since early Thursday."

Dad's forehead wrinkles in confusion. "Hm. That seems a little odd. You haven't talked to him at all?"

"Not since Thursday morning. I tried calling too."

"I'm sorry, sweetheart. How about a drink with your old man?"

I nod and let my dad lead me over to the bar. He orders a glass of his favorite whiskey, and as much as I'd love to drown my sorrows in something much harder, I settle for a glass of white wine.

"There are a few friends I'd like to introduce you to if you're up for it," Dad tells me after he's taking his first sip.

"Of course, let's do this." I plaster on the best smile I can muster as we make our way around the room.

Some of the names and faces are familiar. Others are new to me. Not all of their smiles seem genuine, and for the very first time, I think I can see the devil hiding in some of their eyes.

Have I really been so caught up in the glitz and glam that I've never noticed just how some people can be? I seem to understand even more why my dad's always said keep your friends close and enemies closer. I bet it wouldn't take much for anyone in this room to turn on another.

How many of these people would drop everything to help out a friend or get their hands dirty with something other than lies and deceit?

As the cocktail hour winds down, we make our way to the table we've been assigned for the evening. Senator James MacLeod, his wife Kathleen, and his son Ryan are seated at the table with us and one of dad's Navy colleagues and his wife. The empty chair where Damon should be sitting ironically lingers between me and Ryan.

While the wait staff begins serving appetizers, Mr. Sloan walks on stage and says a few words. He explains how the auction will work and thanks everybody for their support. As he takes his seat, the DJ picks up the music, and chatter takes over the room.

I do my best to make small talk with everyone at the table, thankful that Ryan is kind enough to keep me company when the conversations break off between everyone else.

"May I?" Ryan motions to the chair between us.

"Go for it."

He slides over to the empty chair, so it's easier for us to talk to one another. I've known Ryan long enough to know he's one of the good guys. He's never been my type, though.

"My parents said things are going well for your business. That's good to hear."

"It is. We've been swamped lately. Busy enough that I may even have to hire some more event planners and marketing specialists." I tell him. "How's it going with the law firm?"

Ryan smiles with pride, "It's going well. Rumor has it, I'll be making partner after the holidays."

I give him a friendly side hug. "Congrats, Ryan! That's awesome news. I know you've worked hard for it."

"Doesn't really leave time for much else," his smile drops just a tad.

"I know that feeling all too well," I say with a half-hearted laugh. "Being married to your job doesn't work out well when it comes to relationships."

He shakes his head, knowingly, "it's not totally the other person's fault though, ya know. It's not really fair or good for a relationship when you're caught up in work. Hence why I'm still painfully single."

I'm about to say the same thing when my dad puts a hand on my shoulder and clears his throat.

"I stepped out to use the restroom and found this guy trying to get in," Dad grins and moves to the side.

Damon's entire frame comes into view. If I thought he looked good in a pair of jeans, Damon in a suit is a lot like the most decadent dessert you can imagine.

He's here.

EIGHTEEN
DAMON

Doubt creeps in when I see her hugging the guy sitting next to her.

I didn't drive two and a half hours to get here, swing by Curtis' to change into this goddamn monkey suit and argue with security for ten minutes until Mr. Peterson bailed me out, just to be brushed to the side for some high-class city boy.

"Maeve," her name slips from my lips in a whispered plea. Please tell me I didn't walk in on something I shouldn't have.

"D...Damon?" she stutters and turns to the guy sitting way too close to my girl. "Ryan, if you'll excuse me for a minute." Then she stands up and looks at me. Confusion etches her face. "I didn't think you were coming."

"What do you mean, you didn't think I was coming? I told you I would be here."

"Yeah, well, when I didn't hear from you. I figured you were bailing."

She's clearly annoyed with me. It shouldn't be a turn on, but feisty and headstrong Maeve is pretty hot.

"Babe, I called your office and left a message with Victoria because your cell phone kept going straight to voicemail. I needed to go home and take care of a flu outbreak with the horses. It wasn't something I could leave up to Curtis and Gavin. As it is, I've got to turn around and go back in the morning, but I'm here now, and this is where I want to be."

"Whatever. It's not the time or place. Let's just enjoy tonight, and we can talk about it later."

I straighten my tie and pop the button on the suit jacket. "Sounds good to me."

She turns back around and looks at the Ryan dude. "Ryan, this is Damon. Damon, this is Ryan MacLeod."

Ryan stands and shakes my hand. "Nice to meet you, Damon. Here, have a seat." He moves over one chair closer to an older couple.

Maeve sits first, and I help push in her chair before sitting between her and Ryan.

"Damon, this is my father, Senator James MacLeod, and my mother Kathleen," Ryan kindly introduces the couple to his left.

"Nice to meet you both," I give a nod.

"You already know my dad," Maeve adds. "The couple across the table are friends of his. Jordan Snyder and his wife, Beth. Jordan and Dad serve together."

"Pleasure to meet you both." I stand and shake Jordan's hand as he reaches across the table.

"They should be bringing dinner out in a few minutes. You missed appetizers," Maeve scowls at me.

"I would have been here sooner if not for traffic." I reach under the table and squeeze her knee gently. "The place looks great. You did an amazing job with it."

"Won herself a slot as the event planner for the whole

organization with the job she did for tonight," her dad chimes in proudly.

"That's awesome. That's got to be exciting."

Maeve tries to fight the smile on her face but can't hold back. "I'm still in shock. I don't think I really expected it."

"Psh. Why the heck not? If all your work is this good, I would hire you on the spot too."

She checks me with her elbow. "Flattery will get you everywhere," she whispers with a smirk.

"Good," I wink.

We have a chance to enjoy dinner together before Maeve excuses herself to check on things. Ryan strikes up a conversation with me, and as much as I want to dislike the guy, I can't bring myself to find a good reason to. A whole lot like Mitchell from back home, Ryan is a lawyer – a prosecutor, to be exact.

"I'm sure you see a whole lot of crazy stuff."

Ryan shudders. "Some of it I really wish I could wash from my memory. There's a lot of messed up people in this world, and it's my job to help bring them to justice."

"I commend you. I'm sure it's not for the faint of heart."

He chuckles. "I'm pretty sure dealing with animal crap isn't exactly for the faint of heart either."

"That's what I have ranch hands for," I joke with a shrug. "Grew up that way. It's second nature."

"So, you and Maeve." He changes the subject.

"What about us?" I ask, unsure of what it is he's implying or asking for that matter.

"She's a force to be reckoned with."

"That she is." There's no denying it.

"You two known each other long?" he asks.

"Long enough."

"There aren't farms in DC, so you two doing the long-distance thing?"

I suck my teeth and bit on my lip. "Two hours isn't exactly a long distance. That's a normal commute for some folks."

"True. She's worth it, man. I hope you know that."

"Ryan, I'm really not looking to get into trouble here tonight. You're not going to force me to punch a lawyer, are ya?"

Mr. Peterson laughs behind me and slaps me on the shoulder. Ryan looks nervous for a split second, then he laughs too.

"I think I came off all wrong. Maeve's all yours. I'm only looking out for a friend. That's all. I'm hoping I don't need to hire a hitman to kick your ass then plead the fifth when they can't find your body."

"Alright, boys. No need for a pissing contest," Mr. Peterson warns with amusement. "You both better knock it off because she's headed back this way, and she'll take you both out with one shot."

"I think we're good." I look at Ryan, who shakes his head in agreement.

"Yup. No need to hide two bodies tonight."

Maeve slips into her seat next to me and reaches for her glass of wine.

"Everything okay?" I ask.

"Yup. They're getting ready to open bidding on the auction. Now that everyone has a few drinks, hopefully, they'll be willing to open those checkbooks and add a few zeros at the end."

"It's for a good cause. I'm sure they will. Do you ever bid on anything?" I brush a strand of hair behind her ear, noticing the tiny goosebumps that my touch causes.

"Nah. I let the big spenders do all the bidding."

I may not be as big of a spender as half of the people in this room. That doesn't mean I can't look and make a bid or two in the name of charity. "Hm. What's on the auction block? You want to show me?"

"Sure. You've got to buy me another glass of wine first, though."

"I can do that."

Maeve walks from table to table, introducing me to the volunteers who are manning the auction and looking at each item with me. There's a lot to choose from. Some priced way out of my budget, while others are much more reasonable. I bid on a few of the smaller things knowing that I'll likely get outbid while Maeve insists that I don't need to.

"It's for a good cause. Let me have some fun," I tell Meave as we come across a spa package.

"This place is amazing. My dad bought a massage from here for one of my birthdays. I always said I wanted to go back. Whoever wins this couples package is going to be in for a hell of a treat."

"So, you're saying I should bid on it?"

Maeve shakes her head, "No. God no. Don't do that."

"Maeve. So sorry to interrupt, I need your help for a moment," a woman sweeps her away, leaving me to my own devices.

I place a bid and note my max mid on the bidder's form, then check out the last few items before taking a bathroom break.

When I come back, Maeve's on the dance floor, slow dancing with her dad. I watch the two of them together. Appreciating the bond between a father and daughter.

Mr. Peterson catches me watching and gives me a nod that looks a whole lot like an invitation to cut in. I take his cue and clear my throat when I reach them on the dance floor. "Mind if I cut in?"

He kisses Maeve's cheek, then nods and pats me on the back. "All yours, son."

"Hi," she whispers as I wrap my arms around her and begin swaying to the music.

"I don't think I had the chance to tell you how gorgeous you look tonight."

Her cheeks flush at the compliment. "Thank you. I'm sorry about earlier, you know when you first got here. I was pretty snappy with you."

"Meh. I thought it was hot."

Maeve rolls her eyes at me. "Of course, you did. When I didn't hear from you, I assumed something changed. It sounds stupid in hindsight."

"You don't have to apologize. I did forget to call right away because I was so focused on getting back home. When I saw you called me, it was already after midnight, and I didn't want to wake you, so I tried to get ahold of you yesterday. I promise you that I left a message at the office."

"I believe you. My battery died on my cell phone while I was out and about. I didn't even bother to check messages after I got home since I knew I'd taken care of everything here. Not the most professional move, but I needed sleep," she shrugs. "I'm sure the message is either on my desk or sitting in my emails."

"Well, either way, I'm here now."

"That's what counts," she flashes me a shy smile then leans her head on my chest until the song ends. "Thank you for the dance. I need to go wrap up a few things. Will you wait for me?"

"Absolutely." I grab one last drink from the bar before they close for the evening and head back to the table to wait.

Her father joins me and loosens his tie. "Well, what do you think? Did you enjoy the evening?"

"Yes, Sir. I did. It's an amazing thing they're trying to do, and Maeve's done an amazing job putting this together with everyone."

"She's really good at what she does. That much is for sure," he takes a drink from his glass. "I wouldn't be doing my due diligence if I didn't ask you this, son…What are your intentions with my daughter?"

I nearly choke on my glass of whiskey. I was not expecting that. "Well, we're honestly taking things slow at the moment."

"I thought you may say that," he folds his hands on the table. "Let me let you in on a little secret. Maeve is a tough nut to crack. She's not one to share her feelings so easily, and when she does have feelings? Shew, she'll be the first to push you away."

His words seem awful deep for two people who aren't exactly dating. I probably should have answered his last question a little differently, though I'm not sure how you tell someone's father that you're just fucking their daughter. Hell, even that isn't the complete truth.

"I appreciate the insight," I reply.

"You have no idea why I told you that, do you?" He doesn't wait for me to answer. "Damon, I see the way she looks at you. I heard the way you handled Ryan. Things between the two of you may be brand new, but my girl is falling fast. The last thing I want to see happen is my daughter get hurt."

"Understood. I'm not looking to hurt her."

"No, I don't get the impression that you are. If you have the tiniest bit of doubt about your feelings for her, though, you need to cut her loose before she becomes anymore vested."

"Sir, all due respect, I care about her a lot. Anything more than that should be between me and her when we're both ready to have that conversation."

He nods in understanding. "I can respect that. I've missed out on a lot with my career, but you should know that I can see a difference in her when she's with you. I've never seen her light up like she does now."

"I'll do my best to treasure that." It's a promise I intend to keep.

Maeve walks up behind us both and puts a hand on each of our shoulders, "Good Lord, what are you talking about? You both look so serious right now."

"Man stuff, don't you worry about it," her father pats her hand.

"Jeez. You didn't threaten him with a firing squad, did you, Daddy?" She looks at both of us, I shrug, and her father laughs. "Stupid guy code. As soon as Mr. Sloan announces the auction winners and tonight's grand total, we can go. I'm all finished here after that."

"Sounds like a plan," I tell her and tug her into my lap. "You look exhausted."

A yawn escapes on cue. "It's been a long day."

NINETEEN

MAEVE

"The last item for the night is the ultimate spa package from our good friends at Bethesda Spa. Our winner of this wonderful item with a donation to *No More Sleepless Nights* in the amount of $3253 is Damon Knightly."

An audible gasp escapes. Damon squeezes my hand and winks at me.

"Damon!" I hiss. "You did not."

He shrugs innocently then kisses my cheek. "We should go claim our prize."

Dad laughs at us, "You two go on. I'm going to head out for the night. Behave."

I hug him goodbye, and he gets a handshake from Damon before we got over to the table where the spa package was set up.

"Can I split the cost with you?" I offer.

Damon scoffs while pulling out his wallet. "I'll be damned if I let you pay half."

"You really didn't have to."

"Darlin', you think I don't know that? I did because I *wanted* to." He hands his card over then signs his receipt once it's processed. "Now, what do you say we get out of here?"

"Let's do it."

With the gift certificate for the spa package in hand, we head to the parking lot.

"Did you drive?" Damon asks.

"I did. If you want, you can follow me back to my place."

He thinks for a moment. "I guess we can do that. I was going to go to the townhouse so I can gather the rest of my things. I've got to head back in the morning."

"Oh." I hadn't even considered that he would be going back so soon. "I guess I should go back to my place and let you do that. That's probably a better idea."

Damon wraps his arms around me and pulls me in close. "Did I say I wanted to go back to the townhouse alone?"

"I assumed since you needed to get your things. It's not like I have clothes to change into or anything."

"Then we'll go back to your place. I can get my things tomorrow. I want to spend the night making love to you."

"Oh."

"Yeah, baby. Oh." He growls.

Damon walks me to my car and waits for me to get inside and start it up before he goes to gets his truck and meets me back in front where I'm parked. When we make it to my apartment, he pulls in behind me and is out of his truck to open my door before I even have a chance to turn off the car.

"Have I told you how gorgeous you look tonight?"

"You may have mentioned it," I smile as he takes my hand and leads me inside the building.

We slip into my apartment without a sound, and the first thing I do is kick off the heels that have my feet aching.

"I need a hot shower," I exhale.

He swoops me up in his arms, carrying me to the bathroom. "Then let's get you washed up."

"You don't have to carry me," I laugh and playfully smack his chest to keep from choking up on emotions. It's hard enough knowing that our time together is running out. His affection makes it difficult to keep it together.

Damon sets my feet back on the floor and turns on the shower. Then he gently brushes my hair over my shoulder and slowly drags down the zipper on my dress. It hits the floor at my feet, and I step out while unhooking my strapless bra.

"I need to take this suit off and lay it out flat. I'll be right back," he tells me.

I'm already in the shower, letting the water cascade down my body when he comes back.

"Christ, you're perfect."

"The same could be said about you," I tell him while dragging him under the spray with me.

He pins my hand over my head and kisses me. "I'm going to miss this."

Hearing him saying that out loud has tears stinging my eyes.

"Hey. None of that."

"Maybe we shouldn't do this tonight. I'm not sure I can handle it a goodbye fuck with you."

"Maeve, baby. Is that what you think we're doing?" Confusion itches his face.

"Isn't it? You're going home, and I'll be here. We promised each other a fling. Now our time is up."

He tilts my chin and kisses me softly. "Do you remember when you told me you kinda liked me?"

"Yeah." Of course, I remember. I almost told him I loved him instead. The walls around my heart held it back because I knew this moment right here was coming.

"And I told you I kinda liked you, too."

I nod.

"Baby, I don't just kinda like you. I love you. I can't be too sure when it happened. I know it hasn't been long, but they say when you know – you know. Maeve, I know. I know that I love you. I'm not ready to tell you goodbye. I don't think I'll ever want to say goodbye to you."

My breath hitches in my chest. "What are you saying?"

"I'm saying that I love you, and I want to see where the future takes us. I don't want this to end because I'm going home tomorrow."

"We live two totally different lives, Damon. My life is here. Yours isn't. Don't you think keeping this going is only asking for one of us to get hurt?"

"I'm only two hours away. That's nothing. Hell, I plan to come back here regularly now that Curtis and I are looking into buying a rental property or two. I figured you could come spend some time with me when you've got a day off."

"Eventually, one of us is going to have to make a choice. Damon, I've never lived anywhere but in the city. It's the only life I've ever known. My company is here. My dad is here."

"I'm not asking you to give that up. I'd never ask you to walk away from something you love." He reaches for the shampoo behind me and starts washing my hair. "We're not done talking, but if we don't hurry, we may end up taking a cold shower."

"Mmmhm," his fingers massaging my scalp feels like heaven. I need to focus! "Work is going to get busy now that *No More Sleepless Nights* has come on board. I'm going to have to hire more employees. Free time isn't something I'll have a lot of."

"I know what you're doing. Your dad already filled me in," he smirks. "I get it. We didn't go into this looking for anything more than some fun. If you tell me that you don't feel the same sparks that I do whenever we're in the same room, then I'll walk away. But, if you're being honest, I don't think you can. You're putting up walls because you're afraid of getting hurt. You're not the only one with your heart on the line."

I could kill my father right about now. "Damon."

"Maeve," he challenges me right back. "Tell me I'm wrong."

Searching his face for answers, I can clearly see the love shining back at me. "I love you, too," I finally confess.

His face lights up like a kid on Christmas morning. "That wasn't so hard, was it?"

"No. Let the record show, I still have my hesitations, but I do love you. I can't explain it. Everything with you is so different."

"I'll take it. We can figure out the rest as we go."

With that, we take turns washing each other up and rinsing off. Damon shuts the water off and grabs a clean towel, wrapping me in it before grabbing one for himself.

"I need to dry my hair a little. I won't be able to sleep with it wet like this."

He kisses me then nods. "I'll wait."

It takes me a solid fifteen minutes to dry my hair enough that it's not dripping wet. He's already turned down the sheets and is sitting on the end of the bed waiting for me. Still wrapped in my towel, I go to him.

"Why don't you toss a shirt on? I think I want to hold you for a while."

Damon must be able to see the exhaustion on my face. Now that I'm relaxed from our shower closing my eyes and catching some sleep sounds like a great idea.

"You sure?" I know it's not what he planned.

"I've got plenty of time to make love to you. Let's sleep for now."

It's my turn to kiss him. To tell him how much I appreciate who he is and how he loves me.

He swats my ass and gives me a gentle push, "Shirt now. Unless you plan to sleep naked. I won't complain."

"Hm. I think I like that idea better," I say with a yawn.

"Come on, then." He gets into bed and holds the blankets up for me to crawl under.

I drop the towel and curl up against his warm body, resting my head on his shoulder. "I love you, Damon." This time it comes out in a whisper, yet the words are stronger than before.

TWENTY

MAEVE

"Sarah called to say they settled on a date for their wedding. I responded to an email from a new client interested in putting together a marketing package for her online design company. Oh, and Adele called. She said to let you know she would stop by to see you at lunchtime." Victoria continues to run through her list while I stare out the window and watch the cars roll by.

I can still feel Damon's lips on mine. I can still feel the stubble from his five o'clock shadow between my thighs.

Everywhere I turn, I'm reminded of him. Even at the office, I can still recall lunch with my father. Next thing you know, I'm thinking about the gala and how he showed up when he didn't *have to*. He made it a priority. Made *me* a priority even though he had much more significant responsibilities. The way we slow danced at the end of the night.

My chest tightens, and I rub at the familiar ache, willing it to go away. This is precisely why I didn't want to get involved. It's been a week since I saw him last, and I'm craving him like a drug. Late-night calls and early morning messages are no substitute for the real thing.

"Maeve," Victoria taps on my desk, startling me. "Earth to Maeve. Girl, are you okay?"

I shake my head to clear the memory of our last kiss. "What? Yes. Sorry. I'm fine."

She sits down in one of the chairs across from my desk and sighs. "Girlfriend, he's really got you all messed up. It's like you're not even here."

I can't even argue with her. She's right. I'm so distracted thinking about Damon that I can barely function. I've got it bad.

"You can admit you miss him."

This time I laugh it off and try to regain my composure. "This has nothing with Damon. A lot is going on, that's all."

"If you say so," Victoria shakes her head. "You're not fooling anyone but yourself."

"Ugh. Girl, let it go. I'm not trying to fool anyone." I take the note slips from her, "I'm going to give Sarah a callback. When Adele gets here, you can send her on in."

Victoria nods and stands up from the chair, then stretches her back and runs a hand over her belly.

"Oh, and Victoria? Thank you. For everything. Including putting up with my moodiness."

My assistant smiles back at me. "I've got your back. Always. And now, I need to run to the little girl's room because *someone* keeps dancing on my bladder."

Victoria excuses herself, leaving me to wallow in my own self-pity while I try to focus on work.

Sarah answers on the first ring, giddy with excitement.

"Hey Sarah, it's Maeve. Victoria called and said that you've got a date for the wedding. That's exciting!"

She quickly tells me they've settled on next December, the 12th, giving us well over a year to plan.

"Great. And the venue – you're still interested in either

the Masonic National Memorial, The Smithsonian, or the National Arboretum, correct?"

"Yes, I think we've decided that the Arboretum is on the top of our list because it will look amazing decorated for Christmas. I've already booked appointments with two local bridal shops to look at dresses. Do you have a florist you recommend?" Sarah rattles off at a thousand miles an hour.

I usually love this part of my job. Planning a wedding with an excited bride feels like torture today.

"Perfect. I do have a list of florists. I can schedule appointments with them for us to sit down and look at what they have to offer. I'll call the Arboretum and see if they have the 12th of Dec open and get that booked right away. Is it okay if I email you later today with an update?"

Sarah agrees, and I wrap up our call with a few minutes to spare before lunch with Adele.

Unable to resist, I pull up Damon's name on my phone and send off a dirty message letting him know that I'm thinking of him. He deserves it after the picture he sent to me at six o'clock this morning.

Damon

BULLSHIT.

That's exactly what all of this is anyway.

"No. I don't want the other damn grain. I want the shit I ordered, Mac."

"Damon, I'm sorry. I don't have any in stock."

He's apologized half a dozen times. Too bad. I'm not in the mood to hear it. "How long have I been ordering feed from you, Mac? Tell me when my order has ever changed without notice? I order the same amount of grain every month suddenly, you don't have any to fill that order. What's worse is that you didn't think I needed to know about this until my ranch hand showed up today to pick up everything."

"I don't know what else to say to you. I know we've worked together for years, and I worked with your Dad before that."

"Right, and yet you still couldn't find the decency to call and let me know that you're out of something on my purchase order. You have no idea why you're out of the grain either. You know what. Forget it. I'll call around and find another supplier."

"Damon. Wait!"

Instead of hanging on, I slam the phone down and scroll through the computer for our back-up feed supplier's information.

"Most people come back from vacation in a better mood. You're the only person I know who came back full of piss and vinegar." Gavin says from the doorway of the office.

I pull the ball cap off my head to run a hand through my hair in frustration. "My mood has nothing to do with what you're calling a vacation and everything to do with the fact that now I'm going to have to pay for expedited delivery or send Rawlings clear down to Adamstown, that's if Copeland Feed has enough to fill this order," I grumble.

"And you seem to think that going off on Mac was the answer to solving this problem?"

"Gavin, if you came in here to tell me how to do my job, you should leave before it comes to blows. I'd hate to break that pretty face of yours."

Instead of backing down, he sits across from me and

kicks his feet up onto my desk. "Aww. You think my face is pretty. That's sweet. For the record, I'm not afraid of you. Some of the ranch hands, maybe, though. You keep this shit up, and the new guys will quit by the end of the week."

"Let 'em."

Gavin huffs at me. "Fuck off. We're not letting good help go because you need to get laid."

"I don't need to get laid. Goddamn." Or maybe I do need to get laid. Images of Maeve's body under mine while I pound into her flood my memory. This is insane. Why did I ever think this was a good idea? I'm about to start driving to her house every night after I finish up working just to be next to her.

"Man, I've never seen you this messed up over a girl."

"I'm not messed up over a girl," I lie. There is no way in hell I'm admitting anything to Gavin until I know for sure how it's all going to play out. No one here knows that we're together. "I think being married is turning you into a pussy."

"You've got it bad," he grins at me like a loon.

"I meant what I said about punching you in the face."

"You're not going to punch me in the face. You are going to turn the computer off and leave the grain order until tomorrow and come with me down to Rusty's for a beer or four. Everything else can wait. Rumor has it, Kinsley's single again."

"When is she not?" I snort. "This guy didn't last too long, did he? She was single at your wedding."

"Jesus, don't be a dick. Go on and clean up. I'll be back in an hour with Quinn. Your ass better be ready."

The last damn thing I should be doing right now is going out for beers. With the mood I'm in, public drinking could lead to a whole lot of trouble.

"I see those wheels turning. You're looking for an

excuse. Too bad. I don't want to hear it." Gavin puts his feet down and stands up. "One hour. Go shower; you smell like horse shit."

Knowing he won't leave me alone if I don't go out with him tonight, I give in and head up to the house for a hot shower and fresh clothes. I even have enough time to eat some leftovers that Quinn sent down with Gavin yesterday. With twenty minutes to spare, I dial up Maeve's number. She answers on the first ring.

"Hey, Cowboy."

"Keep calling me Cowboy. I'm going to start calling you City Girl." I tease.

"You act like that would bother me. How was your day?"

"Long. Frustrating. Apparently, I'm an asshole, and I'm scaring off the new help."

"Aww, poor baby. If it makes you feel any better, Victoria called me out for being distracted today."

"Thinking about me again?" I chuckle.

She sighs into the phone. "Maybe."

"I miss you."

"Uh. Damon. Damn you. You shouldn't say things like that."

I know she's teasing, but I also know she's still struggling with the concept of us. Apparently, being with someone who cares so much about her is something that takes getting used to.

"Fine. I won't tell you again tonight."

"Jeez, thanks." She laughs. "What are you getting up to tonight?"

"Gavin's forcing me to get out for a bit. Going to the bar for a drink or two before bringing my happy little ass right back home to go to bed. I got too much shit to deal with tomorrow."

"I'm heading over to *Sip & Sit* in a little bit. Marcie's back in town for a few days."

A little worried about this Justin guy, Maeve took me to her favorite local hang out last week when I came to visit. Turns out Justin is happily married and treats Maeve like his little sister. Now I feel a whole lot better about her hanging out there. It's good to know she's got people looking out for her when I'm not around.

I wish I could stay on the phone longer, but I can see Gavin's truck pulling into the driveway.

"Have fun. Tell the two love birds I said hello. Gavin just pulled up."

"I'll let you go. I love you, Cowboy."

"Love you too, City Girl."

Maeve's laugh lingers in my ears as we hang up the phone.

The drive to *Rusty's Tavern* doesn't take long. Gavin and Quinn grab a table while I order a round of drinks.

We're not at the bar for more than twenty minutes when Kinsley walks in and zeros right in on me.

"Day! It's so good to see you getting out for the night. Gavin said you would be stopping by."

I swallow the last of my beer and look over at Gavin, "Wasn't that so nice of him."

"How was DC? The only time I ever got to visit was when I took a trip to the Smithsonian for an art class in college."

Dear God, help me. "Kins. I don't want to talk about DC."

"Oh," she runs her hand up my arm and squeezes my

bicep. "Well, how about you buy me a drink, and then we can *talk* about us instead."

One beer. I made it through one beer, and I'm ready to go. Where the hell did Kinsley get it in her head that we needed to 'talk' about 'us'?

"Honey, I think you may have already been drinking. You know there is no us."

Now I remember exactly why Kinsley and I stopped fooling around a long time ago. She may be a sweet girl most of the time. Other times she's more than a little crazy and clinging. I'm real damn glad I didn't hook up with her at Gavin's wedding.

"There could be," she whispers in my ear.

"Nope," I quickly stand. "I'm not looking to hook up, Kins. Set your sights on someone else, Hun."

Gavin has the nerve to laugh and gets himself smacked on the back of the head by Quinn.

"You ever try to play matchmaker again; I'll fire you so fast that your head will spin," I warn him with way more grit than I intended. "I'm going the fuck home. Alone."

"Oh, come on, Day. I was only trying to help you out." He defends.

"Then maybe next time you'll listen to me when I say to back off. That'll really help."

"Alright, let's go," Quinn gets up from her bar stool. "I'll take you back home."

"Y'all can stay. I'll walk."

"You can be pissy with Gavin all you want, but you're not walking home. Get your stubborn ass in the truck," Quinn squares off with me. There ain't no winning against her, so I give in and walk my sorry ass on out to their truck.

They drop me off at my house, and I head straight to bed. Sleep doesn't come. I spend the night staring up at the ceiling, thinking about Maeve and how much I wish she were here. Twice I reached for the phone to call her. One look at the time, and I set the phone back down. She would answer, didn't mean it was fair to wake her up when we both gotta get up early and work.

Memories and my hand will have to do for tonight.

TWENTY-ONE

MAEVE

Six weeks later...

Damon: Closing on the rental properties this weekend. Will I get to see you?

Maeve: Client wedding at Martha's Vineyard, remember?

Damon: Damn. Piss poor planning on my part. You did tell me you were going.

Maeve: I'll be home Sunday afternoon if you're still around.

Usually, Damon's messages bring a smile to my face. Knowing that we won't get to see each other this week is enough to make me frown. Every other weekend he's made it a priority to come see me. Some weekends I'm busy working during the day. That doesn't seem to bother him. We still get to spend evenings together, which he swears is better than nothing.

I haven't even had a chance to head north to visit him with all the events on my schedule. The more he tells me about the place he calls home, the more I find myself wanting to, though.

Maeve: Meeting with the bride. I'll catch up with you later on. Love you.

I turn my phone onto vibrate, slip it inside my bag, and then make my way through the hotel to find my bride.

Nicole is sitting at the hotel bar with a bottle of water in her hand.

"Oh, thank God you're here," she hugs me the minute I walk up. "Were you able to get what I needed?"

"Yup. Why don't we go up to my room so you can take care of things?"

She nods and follows me to the third floor. I swipe the key card and let her in before pulling the double pack of pregnancy tests from inside the brown paper bag the drug store gave me.

"I can't believe this is happening right now," her hands shake as she takes the box. "I've always been regular, like clockwork. I should have started two days ago."

"Could be stress from planning. I wouldn't worry too much." I try to assure her from the other side of the closed bathroom door.

I have to say this is the first time I've snuck out for a pregnancy test for a client.

"I'm not so sure." The toilet flushes, and I hear water running as she washes her hands. "We were planning to start trying after the wedding, ya know? So, I've been tracking my cycles. My bachelorette party was exactly 16 days ago. I would have been fertile then."

"Honey, I don't think anyone is going to notice if a little bundle of joy comes along so soon. I bet most people will think it was a honeymoon baby."

"I hope so. I don't want Hudson to be disappointed

either. I don't think we even considered that it would happen so quickly."

While she continues talking, I mentally count back in my head to when my last period was. I know I had one before Damon and I hooked up. That's been...one, two, three, four...oh God, it's been more than four weeks. Way more.

"Oh, thank God!" Nicole squeals and shows me the negative test. "Not pregnant. I'll just leave this one here. You can toss it or whatever. I don't want to tip Hudson off."

"Good idea," I smile weakly.

"And with that, I'm going to the bar for a real drink. I'll see you at the rehearsal later?"

"Yup. I'll be there."

"Thanks, Maeve, you're the best."

"That's why you hired me," I wink and hold open the room door for her.

The door clicks shut behind her, and I pull my phone back out to look at the calendar. Shit. My last period was at the beginning of October. This cannot be happening right now.

I've made it to 28 without ever needing to take a pregnancy test before, not even with any of my long-term boyfriends. I feel like this is a sign from the universe. I swear God has a sense of humor.

The test on the bathroom counter taunts me. I can't believe that now I'm the one freaking out about the possibility of a positive pregnancy test. There's only one way to know.

Three minutes isn't a whole lot of time to alter your future, yet it feels like hours ticking by. I nearly jump out of my skin when the timer on my phone buzzes.

Time's up. I close my eyes and take a deep breath before flipping over the little plastic stick.

Oh shit.

I'm pregnant.

Pregnant.

Breakfast threatens to make a reappearance, and my head feels like it's spinning. I'm having a baby.

I cover my mouth with my hand to muffle the sob that comes out.

I've got to find a way to tell Damon. In person.

Of all times not to bring an assistant with me to an event, it has to be this one. I can't leave, and my flight back home after the wedding isn't until Sunday morning.

It's okay. *It...is...okay.* I'll figure it out. I can go straight from the airport to the townhouse. Damon might still be there, and I can tell him then. Or I can text him right now and ask when he's going back home. Then I would know for sure.

Right. I'll play it cool and see if we can get together when I get back Sunday.

Maeve: You never did answer me. Will you still be in town Sunday afternoon?

He doesn't respond right away, and I eventually have to get to the rehearsal dinner. Dressed in my professional best, I touch up my makeup and head to the restaurant to do my job. My personal life will have to wait.

Damon

MAEVE'S MESSAGE pops up on my screen when I get back in the car after closing on a townhouse a few miles from Curtis.

"We did it. We're officially landlords," Curtis slaps my back.

Turns out, Curtis raised some valid points about fixer-uppers and move-in ready properties. We didn't go with any of the ones Greg showed me, but Curtis was able to find a steal on his own that was perfect.

"I'm glad the current tenants are solid people and agreed to sign a twelve-month lease with us. We should be in the clear for at least the first year."

"Agreed. I think this calls for a little celebration. I made reservations at my favorite steak house. You're going to need to put on a tie, though."

Leave it to Curtis to insist on dinner at a five-star restaurant where I need to wear a damn tie. "I hate you sometimes."

"Did you ever hear back from your lady friend?" He wiggles his brows.

"Shut up. She's out of town. Asked if I was free Sunday afternoon." Curtis was the only one who knew that Maeve and I were still a thing. After the scene at the bar, I figured it was time to tell Gavin.

"Ooo. Does this mean you'll hang around?" he asks.

"Probably."

"Hm. Guess she's worth it."

"Do you really want to get into this right now? Because if we're going to start talking about my love life, then we're talking about why your fiancée is suddenly out of the picture."

"Forget I said anything," he grumbles.

"Seriously. What is it with you two? Every time I

mention talking to you about whatever is bugging you, you get all weird and shut down."

"Day, let it go, man. I'm not interested in talking about it."

"You keep saying that."

"Maybe you should listen." He snarls.

Shaking my head, I respond to Maeve's message and ignore Curtis' grumpy ass.

Damon: I want to see you. What time will you be home?

TWENTY-TWO

MAEVE

This week I beat Dad to the diner. I order some dry toast and ginger ale while I wait to curb the nerves and morning sickness that's starting to creep in.

As usual, Dad's fifteen minutes early, which doesn't even give me time to finish my toast.

"Hey, kiddo. You okay? Upset stomach?" he goes right into protective parent mode.

"Ah, something like that."

He looks me over from head to toe with concern. "Are you going to tell me what's wrong, or are you going to make me guess?"

"Oh, Daddy. I don't think you could guess this one." I hiccup and curse pregnancy hormones when the tears start flowing.

He huffs. "Does it involve Damon? Am I going to have to personally kick his ass for breaking your heart?"

"Uhm. It's a little early to tell on that one," I mumble.

My father scratches his head and passes me a napkin to dab my eyes. "Maeve..." he drags out my name. "You know your old man can be a little dense sometimes. Why don't you just tell me what's going on?"

"I...uhm...we...may have made a mistake. A big one."

"Jesus Christ," he hisses when I won't meet his gaze. "You realize it's not the 1800's anymore, right? Are you pregnant?"

My gaze snaps to his. "Guess you're not as dense as I think you are?" I joke, hoping that the lightheartedness of the moment will ease the tension that I'm feeling.

He gets up out of his seat across from me and slides into the chair beside me instead. "Maeve, sweetheart, for starters – I wouldn't call a baby a mistake. Does Damon know?"

I shake my head. "I haven't had a chance to tell him. I'm driving to his place after breakfast. I want to tell him in person."

"I think that's a good idea. Damon needs to know."

"And what if he doesn't want this baby?" For the first time in days, I feel like I can let my guard down and talk about the fears I've been holding back since I found out.

"Maeve, I don't think a man like Damon is going to turn his back on you or his child."

"Dad, I can't move in with him. How am I supposed to walk away from my life here? You're here. My company is here. The company that I built from the ground up. I won't give that up."

"Slow down, kiddo. One thing at a time," he rubs my back. "I'm always going to be in your corner, but we all know that if I land this next position, it may come with a new stop on the map. You can't live your life based on mine. Besides, when this kiddo comes into the world, your whole perspective is going to change. Trust me on that."

"It didn't change for you," the words slip out before I

have a chance to stop them. Blame the hormones for making me crazy and bitchy.

"Oh, but it did. Maeve, when you were born, I almost walked away from the Navy. Your mom begged me to give it up. If not for a hard dose of reality from Tillie, I probably would have. What did I have to offer a newborn baby if I walked away from my career? I just graduated from the Naval Academy and was already assigned my first duty station. I owed the Navy at least four years. The pay wasn't great, but I had health insurance. Your momma wasn't willing to wait four years, and at that point, you were doing so well with Tillie. If I stayed, I knew I could make a better life for you. So that's what I did."

"Daddy, I didn't mean that." I sniffle. "I'm sorry."

"I'm not worried about it, baby girl. My point is, we all make choices. Sometimes they come with regrets, and sometimes they come at the cost of our hearts. If I could do one thing over again, I would have found a way to make it work with your momma. After she left, I closed off my heart and focused on the job. What I got out of that was an amazing woman who grew up thinking that the world is better alone. Don't get me wrong. I'm damn proud of the woman you've become. But trust me when I tell you that life is so much better when you can share it with someone you love."

Wiping the tears from my eyes, I nod in agreement. "I'm such a mess."

"I'm told that's normal," he winks. "Let's get you fed so you can go tell that man of yours that he's going to be a daddy."

I nurse my toast until our usual order arrives. I force down a few bites of eggs for substance, hoping they won't come back up later. While we eat, Dad reminds me that there's still a world of opportunity out there for me.

"You know, there's no reason why you couldn't spend some time at Damon's place. Try to telework from there. Maybe scout a few places in the area that might be a good place to set up shop. How long have you been talking about wanting to eventually expand? I happen to know that there's at least one gal on your team who would slip into a manager's role quite well. She could cover things here and it's not like it's so far away that you can't come back and check in on things."

"I think I need you to stop being so logical," I tell him halfheartedly. I kinda hate when he has a valid point, especially when I didn't think of it first.

"Before I stop being so logical," he winks at me. "You also need to give Damon a fair shot. If you're not all in with him, you're never going to know if it's meant to be."

I gasp in shock. "I am all in with him. Dad, we're having a baby. There's not much more all in than that."

"Child. Having a baby doesn't mean you're all in. It only means things are moving a whole lot faster. If you were all in, your sassy little independent tail would have already been to visit him before now instead of making that man come to you every single time."

"I thought you were on my side."

"I am on your side. Always. Remember what I said earlier, though. It's not the 1800's anymore. You're his equal. Love and relationships should be 100% all the time. You both have to give it your everything.

My father's words of truth sting. He's right.

At least after talking with him, I feel remotely better about breaking the news to Damon later.

MY LITTLE TOYOTA COROLLA stirs up dusk along the gravel driveway before I come to a stop in front of a gorgeous rancher. Damon's pick-up truck is parked beside the house, and the front door is open. It's only two in the afternoon on a Saturday. He has no idea that I was coming, so I'm not sure where I'll find him.

This week, I spent every day moving my schedule around and delegating work so I could take some vacation time. For the first time since I started the company, I'm taking a solid week off.

The secret I've been keeping all week is nearly eating me alive. I can only hope that it doesn't send Damon running for the hills.

Pulling all the courage I've got, I shut off the car and step out on to the Pennsylvania clay.

I haven't even closed my car door when Damon steps out onto the porch and covers his forehead to block the sun. "Something I can help you..." he pauses then blinks slowly. "Maeve?"

"Hi."

He takes the front porch steps two at a time and meets me halfway.

"You're here." Damon runs his thumb over my cheek like he's checking to make sure I'm real.

"I'm here."

"I thought...You said..." he shakes his head. "What are you doing here?"

"Well, you talked about how much you loved living here. I just had to see for myself what the fuss was all about."

He smiles and picks me up in his arms to twirl me around. "Never in my wildest dreams did I think you would actually show up here."

I'd give anything to hang on to this moment a little longer, but I can't. "We should talk."

Damon's body stiffens. "Well, shit. That doesn't sound good."

Way to go, Maeve. Cut right to the chase and terrify the poor guy. "It's not bad. Well, not exactly. Guess it depends on how you feel about what I need to tell you."

"Come on inside. We can talk about whatever's on your mind," he holds my hand as we walk up the front porch steps and into his house. "Have a seat," Damon extends his arm, welcoming me into the living room.

I sit down on the couch, and Damon takes a seat on the coffee table so that he's directly across from me and leans forward so that he's still touching me.

"So. Uhm. Well. I know you said one day...I'm not so sure how you'll feel about this..." All of the thoughts in my head are jumbled together. Anxiety is getting the best of me. I can't even find the right words to say.

"How I feel about what exactly?"

"We never really talked about raising babies and marriage."

"Maeve, did you drive all the way here to ask me to marry you?" Damon grins playfully.

"Oh, my God. No." I hadn't even considered that he would probably want to get married once he finds out I'm pregnant. Talk about going from 0 to 180. My face pales, and my palms start sweating.

"Breathe. I was kidding. Take a deep breath."

I can't. I need to rip the bandaid off and come right out and say it. "Damon. I'm pregnant."

His eyes widen, and he swallows hard. "Pregnant."

"Looks like you're going to be a dad." I try to smile even though I feel like throwing up.

Damon runs a hand over his face and blows out a breath. "We're having a baby?"

"Surprise?"

"Holy Shit," he stands and paces around.

"My thoughts exactly."

When he comes to a stop in front of me, he kneels and puts both of his hands on my knees. "You're having my baby?"

I can't blame him for being shocked. I had an entire week to get used to the idea, and I still have moments where it doesn't seem real.

"I am," I reach into my purse and pull out the ultrasound picture from yesterday. "Seven weeks and three days to be exact."

He looks at the image and back at me. "Wow. We're having a baby." This time tears fall from his eyes, and he wraps his arms around me. "I love you, Maeve Peterson. So goddamn much. I can't believe I'm going to be a dad."

"Still processing the fact that I'm going to be a mom," I confess.

Damon looks me in the eyes, "We'll figure it all out together."

"I don't want you to feel like we have to run off and get married or anything crazy. The baby doesn't change any of that."

"Sweetheart, a baby changes everything. I respect what you're saying, and I'll wait until you're ready. But you should probably start getting comfortable knowing that one day you are going to wear my ring and be my wife."

"Damon." I give him a warning glare that he ignores in favor of picking me up and twirling me around again.

"We're having a baby," he kisses my cheek. "I've never been so goddamn happy."

This time his words sink in. I'm relieved. All the stress and worry over the last few days about telling him. The fear of him balking at the idea. It's slowly fading out the window.

We'll have to figure out so many logistics, like where to go from here. At least I know I'm not doing this alone.

The sound of the backdoor opening startles me. Boots stomping on the floor, and an unfamiliar voice breaks up our moment too soon.

"Alright, asshole, you said you'd be back in ten minutes. Where the fuck are..." another guy dress much like Damon in a t-shirt, and worn jeans comes into the living room. Looking at his face, I realize that he was one of the guys in the photo that Damon showed me from his buddy's wedding.

"You must be Gavin," I wipe my hands on the front of my jeans and then offer to shake his hand.

A cocky grin spreads across his face. "Well, I'll be damn. I'm going to guess that you're the woman who's got my boy here all tied up in knots." He takes my hand and kisses the back of it like I'm some fairy princess while laughing his ass off when Damon steps between us.

"Hands off, or I'm telling Quinn," Damon growls.

"Now I know what was taking you so long. Guess you're done for the day."

Damon looks at me. "I got a few things to finish up. You're sticking around, right?"

"If you'll have me."

Gavin laughs. "Oh, hell. If you'll have her. Bless her heart."

"Gavin. Get the fuck out." Damon points to the backdoor.

I'm surprised when he does exactly as he's told and leaves us alone again.

Damon cups my face and kisses me. "That's not even a question. You're mine. What's mine is yours, and you're damn right, I want you here."

The dam that has been holding back all of my tears finally break. "I love you, Damon. I was so scared that you wouldn't want this or you'd be upset. We didn't plan it, and..."

"Hey, hey, hey...It's okay. It's all going to be okay. You're here right now, and we'll figure out the rest. I've got you." He wipes my tears away and lets me bury my head in his chest until I start gagging and laughing at the same time.

"You smell like cow shit."

He chuckles and backs up. "Sorry. Took you long enough to notice."

"I think I tuned it out," I gag again.

"Let me go finish up, then I'll shower. Make yourself at home. I shouldn't be too much longer."

"Go. Please," I cough out.

While he gets back to work, I locate the bathroom to wash my face and try to get rid of the stench that has infected my nose.

Wandering out onto the back porch, I notice a porch swing that looks like the perfect spot to curl up and soak in the fantastic view of the countryside.

TWENTY-THREE
DAMON

"Guess we're all going to have to deal with that goofy-ass grin on your face as long as she's here." Gavin jokes while we finish loading hay up into the loft.

"I wouldn't be talking. You still have that love-struck look on your face every day." I dish it right back at him.

"You say that like it's a bad thing," he huffs. "I do gotta say though, seeing you two together, it all makes sense."

"What makes sense?"

Gavin shakes his head at me. "You're in love, dumbass."

I rub the back of my neck and shrug, "I already knew that."

"So, what finally brought her here? Do you think she can handle this kind of life?"

"Turns out we had some things to talk about," I can't fight the proud grin on my face. "and given what she told me; I hope like hell she can handle living here at some point."

My best friend stares at me in shock. "You got her knocked up, didn't you?"

"He did." Maeve's soft voice chimes in.

When I turn around, she's standing in the barn watching us.

"Maybe it's Damon who needs to learn to live in the city," this time her words are clipped, and I know she heard what I said.

Moving to the city never crossed my mind. Hell, I know I told her I wouldn't ask her to give up her life there. I meant it then when I wasn't expecting a child of my own. I always thought I'd get married and settle down to raise a family here. The thought of living somewhere else never crossed my mind.

Being the intuitive fucker that he is, Gavin tells me he'll finish up. I wipe my hands on the towel hanging from my pocket and nod.

"You up for a little tour?" I ask Maeve.

She shakes her head at me and pins her nose with her fingers. "Not until you've showered."

"Wanna help me wash my back?"

"That's a no." She grins and follows me back up to the house. "I didn't mean to pull you away from work. I was sitting on the porch swing and taking it all in. I guess I got curious and followed the voices once I got closer."

"It's okay; you can admit you can't resist me."

"Pretty sure that's what got us into this situation."

I can't tell if she's upset by that or not, but when I turn to look at her, there's mischief twinkling in her eyes. "Har har, smartass. Come on, I'll show you the master bedroom. Who knows, maybe you'll change your mind and join me in the shower."

She stops at the doorway and looks around while I strip out of my clothes. I don't miss her grumble when I leave them all in the middle of the floor. "It's nothing fancy, but it works for me," I tell her about the space.

The king-size bed is made from solid wood and build with my own two hands. The linens are a plain gray that match the curtains. There's one picture on the dresser of my whole family from Gavin's wedding. Other than that, it's pretty void of any décor.

"It's simple. Like you." She murmurs quietly.

"Is that a bad thing?"

"No," she rolls her eyes. "I like you just as you are."

I move in for a kiss, "You *love* me."

Maeve backs away. "Shower. Please."

"Fine," I chuckle on my way to the en suite.

Freshly showered and dried off, I walk out of the bathroom ten minutes later, completely naked.

Maeve is standing at the window looking out onto the back of the property.

"That view never gets old."

She jumps at the sound of my voice and turns toward me. One look at me, and she bites her lip. "I think I like this view better."

Goddamn. My cock jumps at the notion.

"Do you know how long I've dreamed about having you here? How many nights I've woken up with my hand wrapped around my cock, thinking about making love to you in *my* bed?"

"I think you should show me."

That's all I need to hear. One swift kick shuts the bedroom door. If Gavin hasn't left yet, he won't be too much longer. He may have enough sense to not come back up to the house, but I'm not taking any chances.

Maeve meets me in the middle of the room. Her hands on my skin are the sweetest torture and the best salve to my soul.

"I've missed you so much." She whispers against my lips.

"I've missed you, too. So, damn much."

"Make love to me."

Taking my time with her, I do exactly what she asks.

From head to toe, I worship her body until she's shaking and begging for more. The minute my cock is finally buried inside her, I'm able to breathe again for the first time in weeks. Feeling her underneath me, knowing she's here and this isn't a dream, unravels me until we're both panting and gasping for air. Maeve goes first, screaming my name as I follow behind her into oblivion. When the throbbing stops, I lay down beside her with one arm holding on to her.

"Damon."

"Hm."

"I'm scared." The tiny hitch in her voice pulls at my heart.

"It's unchartered waters. I get it. I'm not going anywhere."

"I don't want our baby to grow up in two separate homes, ya know?"

I lean up on my elbow and look at her. "I don't either."

"I'm afraid that moving here would mean giving up my dreams."

"I'm not here to take your dreams away. Maeve, I want to help you keep chasing those dreams."

"Please don't be mad. I talked to my dad about everything at breakfast today."

"Why would that make me mad? He's your father. Wait. He's not going to kill me, is he?"

Maeve lets out a laugh. "No. He promised he wouldn't kill you. Honestly, he was pretty okay with becoming a grandpa. He said some things that made sense. Things that I should really think about. He also said that I really need to give us a fair shot."

"Your dad is a smart man. I don't know if you know that or not."

She playfully punches my arm. "I figured you would say that. You know, he really likes you."

"I'm glad I've somehow managed to earn his respect."

"Do you really want me to move here?"

There it is. The million-dollar question.

"I always thought I would be raising a family here," I reply with the best answer I can give her.

"What if I kept my apartment in DC for a little while?"

"Then I'll hire help around here to pick up my slack so I can be with you more."

She shakes her head at me. "No. That's not exactly what I meant. I'm not planning to pack up and move today. I don't even know if I can stomach the smell."

That causes me to throw my head back, and full-on belly laugh. "I'm sure you'll eventually get used to it."

Maeve doesn't seem convinced. "I wouldn't be so sure. Not with morning sickness to consider too. Anyway, I meant, could we keep the apartment to maybe have a little getaway once in a while. Let's say I do move here. It would be nice to have an escape for the two of us when I'm craving the city. Or when I go back for work."

My free hand has already made its way to her belly. It's hard to believe there's a little bean already growing inside of her. "Is the morning sickness awful?"

She puts her hand over mine. "Is that all you gathered from that conversation?"

"Nope. I heard you say you're moving here."

"Damon! That was not what I said!"

"Give it time, City Girl. Give it time."

TWENTY-FOUR

MAEVE

Waking up in Damon's bed is surreal.

How can something that I swore I didn't want, feel so right?

The alarm clock shows it's a little after nine. His side of the bed is empty, but the smell of coffee fills the air. Pulling on his t-shirt from the night before, I pad down the hallway and into the kitchen only to come to a screeching halt when forks clamor against the dishes and six sets of eyes meet mine. Like a deer in headlights, I'm frozen in place.

"Maeve." Damon jumps up so fast that his chair tips over onto the floor. His hands on my shoulders guide me backward away from prying eyes.

"Oh, God." Mortification kicks in. All I want to do is run and hide.

"I forgot to tell you that I usually have breakfast with my ranch managers on Sunday mornings."

I can't even look at him right now.

"I'd like the earth to swallow me whole, please." I squeak out.

Damon snorts.

Gavin yells in from the kitchen, "Don't worry, we didn't see...much."

"Fuck you!" Damon yells back then looks at me. "Go change. I'll make sure they're gone before you get back."

I can't believe I just walked into a kitchen full of cowboys in nothing but a white t-shirt. Fuck. I don't think I'm cut out for this.

Locked safely behind the bedroom door, I quickly change into a pair of jeans and my own shirt – with a bra on underneath. Then I stall for as long as I can, too afraid to come face to face with any of Damon's buddies anytime soon.

A few minutes later, there's a knock on the door. I can hear the rumble of Damon's laughter on the other side. "Let me in, City Girl."

I flip the lock and open it enough for him to slip through.

"This is not funny," I pout.

"The coast is clear. I made them all swear to never mention a word about what happened, too."

"That doesn't make me feel any better. Why didn't you warn me?"

He shrugs like the smug asshole that he is. "I didn't think about it. It's our normal routine around here. Having you here feels just as natural. The thought never crossed my mind that you didn't know they would be here."

"Yeah, well, it's a good thing that shirt covered all the good parts!" I lower my voice and whisper, "I wasn't wearing panties."

Damon's eyes darken, "I'm buying you a robe. No more Sunday breakfasts either. Fuck that."

"Oh, five minutes ago, you thought this was hilarious." I pretend that I'm upset and cross my arms across my chest.

"That was before you said you were not wearing panties."

"Mmhmm. Sure."

"Wish I didn't have a full schedule today. I'd bend you over the dresser and show you what happens when you walk around like that."

I raise a brow, "Really? What's stopping you?"

"You. I need to feed you and get you fueled up with coffee. Then we need to go to the store before I get to work."

"Who said I was going to the store?"

"The second rule when you're here...You need to have boots on if you're going to wander around."

I huff. "And the first rule?"

"Only I can see you in my shirts. Scratch that. Boots is rule number three. Second rule is no panties."

"I'll agree to rule number one and number three. I'll decide when and where to forgo undergarments. Thank you very much."

Damon scoops me up and wraps my legs around his waist. "We'll see about that too."

He carries me through the house, every step causing an ache between my legs and my breath to hitch.

"You okay?"

"Wipe that look off your face. You know damn well what you're doing." I scold him as he sits me down at the kitchen table.

There's already a full plate and a cup of coffee waiting.

"You can still have coffee, right?"

"A cup a day."

"Good," he kisses my cheek. "I'm running out back to check in on a few things. Be right back." He heads for the backdoor and stops with his hand on the knob. "Hey, Maeve."

"Hm."

"I like having you here." He doesn't give me a chance to respond before he disappears.

I'm left on my own to eat breakfast with a goofy grin on my face.

GOING into town was exactly as Damon described it. A few miles down the road, the countryside gave way to a tiny little main street with shops lining both sides and a church nearly right in the center of it all. I could already picture how it must look in the winter when snow covers the ground. It was vastly different from the center of DC, but its quaintness drew me in like a postcard.

Today in the passenger seat, I really have a chance to take it all in. I missed the entire thing yesterday, on my mission to get to Damon.

"Alright, the first stop is *The Tack Shop*. They're really creative with their names for things around here," He winks at me while pulling into a parking spot. "Sit tight. I'll get your door."

Determined to ruffle his feathers, I ignore him and open my own door. The look on his face as I climb down from his truck is priceless.

"Are we playing a different game now that we're on my home turf?"

Doing my best to keep a straight face, I shrug at him. "Depends. Do you really think that I'm going to let you open my door every time we go somewhere?"

"Lord, I've got my hands full," he shakes his head. "I'm gonna end up get my ass whooped because you need to be all independent and shit."

"Well, if it isn't Damon Knightly," a voice calls out as we step onto the sidewalk.

I nearly laugh out loud when I see who appears to be the Sherriff walking toward us. I feel like I'm on the set of a *Hallmark* movie, a walking cliché of small-town life.

"Bobby, didn't I see you what, two days ago?" Damon shakes hands with him and turns to me. "This is Maeve. Maeve, this is Bobby McCallister. He thinks he's the Sherriff's Deputy. We haven't bothered to tell him that badge is make-believe."

"Ignore him," Bobby gives my hand a shake. "Is this the lady that the whole town has been talking about?"

"Talking about?" I question. "I haven't been here twenty-four hours yet!"

"Ma'am, they saw you roll through here going about fifty-five in a thirty-five. I almost pulled you over yesterday until I saw you turn off onto that dirt road leading back to Day's place."

"I was not going fifty-five." At least, I don't think I was.

"My hand on the Bible," Bobby replies.

Damon has the smarts to keep a straight face when I look at him.

"Well, in that case, I apologize for breaking any laws. That wasn't my intent."

"Naw, don't worry about it. Damon's probably gotten more tickets for speeding through here than anyone else in this town."

"You mean, gotten away with it more than anyone else. I don't think you've written me a ticket one time, Bobby."

"True story."

Bobby's radio crackles to life, and he excuses himself to take care of a cow stuck in the road.

"How exactly is the Sherriff's Deputy going to arrest a cow?" I ask innocently.

This time Damon chuckles. "He's not going to arrest the cow. Bessy gets out once a week. We all think it's because she likes to see Bobby. He's learned how to bribe her back onto her side of the fence."

"Interesting."

Outside *The Tack Shop,* I wait and let Damon open the door for me. I'm rewarded with a swat on the ass and that dimpled smirk that I love so much.

"Hey, Mac," Damon calls out to the guy behind the counter. If I had to guess, he looks to be about my father's age or older. I can't help but wonder if he's the store's original owner or if, like Damon's farm, it's been passed down through generations.

"Glad to see you're in a better mood." Mac answers.

Damon's ears turn red, a trait that I've never noticed about him before. "I said I was sorry. You still mad at me?"

"If I was, I wouldn't have ordered all these," Mac nods to several boxes of boots. "Besides, I told you, you had a point. I let that guy go for screwing things up. I don't have time for stuff like that. All your orders have been right since then, haven't they?"

"Yeah, they have."

"Good. I grabbed a chair for you and set it at the end of the counter. Let me know which ones you decide to go with," Mac tells him, then goes back to whatever he was doing behind the counter.

"Damon, how many pairs of boots do you think I need?"

He kisses my forehead, a move that I'm beginning to learn is his way of calming me down or getting me to bend to his well-meaning way of thinking.

"Two or three at the most. They each have a different purpose, and they all fit differently."

"Do I even want to know how you know my shoe size?"

"I might have looked in your closet. Planned on buying you a pair for your birthday or something."

Several pairs of boots later, we've managed to narrow it down to two. One for around the farm and another for 'going out.' Damon tried to talk me into a third pair. One glimpse at the price tag and I refused.

"Got what you need?"

"Sure do. Thanks for ordering those in. You sure it won't be a problem if you need to send them back?" Damon asks while Mac rings us up.

"Send them back? I ain't sending those back. My nephew has an online store for this place. He'll list them on there, and they'll be gone by the end of the week," he scans the second pair of boots. "That'll be $368.21. You want me to put this on your account?"

"No." We both answer at the same time.

Damon glares at me with a silent warning. "You can put your wallet away."

"Nope. What I can do is pay for my own shoes." I try to bump my hip against his and knock him out of the way, but he remains cemented in place with his arms now crossed over his chest and one brow raised.

"Put them on my personal account," Damon tells Mac and grabs both boxes off the counter. "Do me a favor too, let everyone know this one's money isn't good here. Anything she wants gets billed to me."

He trudges out the door, making sure to hold it open for me.

Mac chuckles. "You better go on. You're not going to win against any of the Knightlys, Hon. No use in trying."

I huff and go after Damon.

"You do not have to go around buying me things!" I stomp my foot and point a finger at him. "I could have bought those."

"I said they were a birthday gift," he keeps right on walking and opens up the truck door for me. "Get in."

"No."

Damon looks over his shoulder at me. "Maeve, what the hell are you doing? Get in the truck."

"No. I'm not getting in the truck until you let me go back in there and pay for those boots, Damon."

He tosses the boxes behind the seat and walks over to me. "I don't know if it is our baby making you so feisty or if you're finally getting comfortable with me. Either way, I like it." He hauls me up over his shoulder and carries me to the truck.

I retaliate by pinching his non-existent love handles and nearly end up being dropped. He grunts, and I squeal. A few passerby's watch like we've both lost our minds as Damon somehow manages to sit me on the passenger seat. He buckles me in like I'm a child, then shuts my door, waving to everyone who's watching as he walks around the truck.

The humor written all over his face as he backs out of the parking spot is enough to get under my skin in more ways than one.

"I'm giving you that money back," I insist.

"You're not. I said I already planned on buying you a pair for your birthday or whatever."

"You don't even know when my birthday is! And you said ONE pair. At least let me pay for the other pair!"

"Your birthday is November 25th, a week from today. It was on your *Love Bites* profile. Give me a little credit here."

"Okay, fine! Still, one pair is enough."

"Maeve, we can argue over the boots all damn day. You're still not paying for them, so get over it."

"Ugh."

"Ugh," he mocks me.

"You're a pain in the ass, Cowboy."

TWENTY-FIVE

DAMON

"You're not mucking stalls. I said you could take a tour. I did not say you would be doing chores."

Note to self: Maeve *can* stay mad at me over some boots all day.

I probably shouldn't be so turned on by her attitude either.

"Fine, then let me feed them." She huffs at me for what must be the thousandth time today.

"No. The feed containers are heavy."

She darts to my left to try and get around me. "Damon, I'm not going to break."

"Maeve," this time, I manage to catch her around the waist and pull her against me. She lets out a squeal then shivers when I nip her ear. "I never said you would break. You're carrying my goddamn child. You don't belong out here doing grunt work. You want to do something productive, I'll let you collect eggs from the chickens in the morning."

She wiggles her ass against my cock that's been hard all

day thanks to her. I'm about two seconds from dragging her inside my office and spreading her out on the desk when Gavin walks in with Rawlings.

"Hm. Ain't no wonder nothing is getting done around here," Gavin smarts. "You can't keep your hands off the lady long enough to get anything done."

Maeve untangles herself from my grasp and straightens her shirt. "Yeah, well, we'd get a lot more done if he'd let me help."

"No can do, Lady. I'm with Day on this one. At least not right now." Gavin backs me up with a knowing look.

"You're all frustrating egotistical buttholes."

Rawlings doubles over in laughter. "She called y'all buttholes."

"Shut up," she points right at him. "You're one of them too."

"Hey, I was going to give you some work to do," he offers.

"No, you were not." Gavin slaps the back of his head.

"If you want to keep your job, you will do no such thing. Are we clear?" I add.

"Fine. We're clear," Rawlings holds up his hands. "I'm finished for the day. You want my help in here before I head out?"

"Nothing I can't handle. Thanks."

"See you in the morning," he tips his ball cap before he leaves.

The sound of metal scraping on the ground diverts my attention. Gavin and I both turn to find Maeve in the stall with Sandi, shoveling horse shit into a pile.

"Goddamnit, Maeve."

Of course, Gavin finds the entire thing funny.

"Woman. Stop for two seconds and listen," I warn her as I step into Sandi's stall and take hold of her harness. Thank fuck Sandi is the most easy-going horse on this farm; otherwise, this stubborn woman of mine could find herself in a lot of trouble.

"Maeve, he's serious." Gavin comes over with Sandi's lead in hand.

Finally, she seems to listen and stops moving.

"You can't muck the stall with the horse in it," I do my best to keep the tone of my voice even while I clip Sandi's lead on. "Stand still," I warn her before clicking my tongue at Sandi. "Walk." Sandi does as she should and walks out of the stall with me. "Do me a favor and keep her out of trouble for five seconds while I put this one outside," I tell Gavin.

I walk alongside Sandi and run one hand down her cheek, sweet-talking her for staying calm and not kicking or biting Maeve. She sputters like she understands and moves her head up and down. When I get her to the field, I open the gate and walk her inside before removing her lead. "Good girl." She lets me pet her one more time before she takes off to do her thing.

The last thing I expect to see when I walk back into the barn is Maeve sitting on a hay bail in tears and Gavin shoveling out Sandi's stall. Rushing to her side, I kneel and check her over. "Are you okay? What happened?"

"I'm fine," she sobs. "I didn't know she could hurt me."

"Yesterday, the smell of 'cow shit' as you called it, was enough to make you sick. Today you want to shovel shit with a horse still in the stall." I brush her hair back from her face. "Maeve, there's a way to do things around here that doesn't involve anyone getting hurt."

"Yeah, well, I wouldn't have tried to do it on my own if you had taken the time to show me."

I let out a deep breath. "I never said I wouldn't show you. I said you were not going to be *doing* any of the work. You can watch all you want."

"That's not fair."

"Think of this way, how would you feel if I walked into your office or a wedding that you spent all this time planning and just jumped in with no prior experience?"

She pulls the end of her shirt up to wipe her eyes. "I'd probably kill you."

"Good, then I think you can understand what I'm getting at. You can't waltz in here and think that you can jump in and help out with no understanding of how things are done. Especially around thousand-pound animals. Don't even get me started over the fact that you don't need to be shoveling shit or carrying around feed buckets while you're pregnant."

Maeve chokes back another sob. "I feel like a basket case. First, you wouldn't let me pay for my own boots, then you wouldn't let me help out. It all made me feel helpless."

"Jesus Christ. I know you're not helpless. I'll tell you what, if you don't hush about the boots, I'll go back and buy the other pairs that you liked and fit well."

That gets her complete attention. She looks up at me with pure fire in her eyes. Every tear has stopped. "You wouldn't," she hisses at me.

"He would!" Gavin calls out. "I hate to break up your little moment over there. I've got my own woman waiting on me at home, so if the two of you could kiss and make up so Damon can help me with the rest of these stalls, I'd appreciate it."

Maeve leans a little closer to me and whispers, "Is he always like this?"

"Yes," I chuckle. "Come on, I'll *show* you how this is supposed to be done. If you can play nice, I'll let you carry the empty buckets."

TWENTY-SIX
MAEVE

After a complete meltdown yesterday, where I really did act like a total basket case, I swore I would pull myself together and do better today. Starting with *not* walking out of the bedroom wearing next to nothing.

This morning the house is tranquil and empty. In the kitchen, I find a note on the coffee pot and a clean cup sitting beside it.

Morning City Girl,

Left your breakfast in the oven. It may still be warm.

Working on repairing a piece of fence today. I'll try to come back around lunchtime to check on you. Call or text me if you need anything. There shouldn't be any visitors at the house today, but you might want to keep your clothes on, just in case. Please stay out of trouble. ::winky face::

Love you,

Damon

I hug the note to my chest while looking out the back window. I don't think he has to worry about me causing any trouble today. Our long talk last night in the bath was more than enough for me to get my head on straight, especially after what Damon said in the barn about jumping headfirst into a job I knew nothing about.

Finally, tucking the note into my pocket, I fix a cup of coffee and pull the warm plate of food from the oven. While I eat, I send Damon a text to ask for the wi-fi password. I promised Victoria and Autumn that I would check in on them today, and I'm sure I've got things I could work on until lunch.

His reply dings two minutes later.

Damon: We don't have wifi.

I'm about to call him a liar when another message comes thru.

Damon: I'm kidding. It's KnightAlpha83

Maeve: I was about to pack my bags and go home. No wifi is a deal-breaker.

Damon: I guess it's a good thing that we joined the 21st century then. Did you find the note I left?

Maeve: Yes. Thank you. I love you too.

Damon goes silent after that. I finish up my breakfast, clean up the dishes, and then head back to the bedroom to pull out my laptop. Once I'm logged in, I give Victoria a call.

"Pretty sure we told you there was no need to call," she answers on the first ring.

"Pretty sure, I'm the one who gives out orders around here," I joke. "How are things?"

"Maeve, it's only been an hour since the day started here. We're fine. How is it there? Was he surprised to see you?"

Victoria has no idea about the real reason that I decided to make this visit happen. Now that Damon knows, I could tell her even though it's still pretty early on.

"He was surprised, alright. Just about as surprised when I told him we are having a baby."

She squeals so loud that I have to hold the phone away from my ear. "Oh my gosh! I knew it!"

"Hey. Slow down. And keep your voice down, please. I don't want everyone to know yet."

"My lips are sealed."

"Wait. What do you mean, you knew it?" Did everyone in my life seem to know this before I did?

"I manage your calendar, duh."

That's all she has to say for me to realize that she saw the slot for my doctor's appointment from Friday. "Is pregnancy brain really a thing, and does it happen this early?"

"Honey, it's real. Happens right along with the mood swings and vomiting."

"Speaking of mood swings, Vic, I wish you could have seen me yesterday." With Victoria now in the know, I recount every detail from the boots to mucking the stalls and sobbing like a moron.

"Sounds about right," she giggles. "You just wait. It gets better. Wait until your sex hormones go into overdrive."

I nearly spit out the water was trying to drink. "Please tell me that you're talking about this with me at your desk."

"Hell no. I'm in your office. I came in here to grab a phone number for one of our vendors when you called. I already shut the door, too. No one can hear me."

"Victoria, put my pens back. You're not fooling me." For as long as she's worked for me, Victoria has a vengeance for stealing my pens, claiming that they're better than the ones I buy for the rest of the staff. "You have your own."

"These still write better."

"They're the same damn pens," I roll my eyes.

"Whatever. How did Cowboy react to your being all crazy yesterday?"

"Uhm. Let's just say we worked it out by the end of the night."

"Yes, girl! That's what I'm talking about. Oh, hey, you know that the schedule is pretty much empty next week, too, right? You should just take an extra week and spend Thanksgiving with your boo thang."

"Please do not ever refer to Damon as my boo thang again. I need to come home and spend Thanksgiving with my dad."

"Uhm. Pretty sure he would tell you to stay put. Just saying. I mean, why the hell not. We have one event on Autumn's schedule. Everyone else is off. There's nothing that you can't handle from there."

"I'll think about it. Listen, while I've got you on the phone...Are you really planning on coming back after you have the baby?"

"Maeve, it's like you don't even know me at all. Yes, I plan to come back after this little one is born. I love all my kids to death, but I know I am not cut out to be a stay at home mom. Why?"

"What would you say if I told you that I was thinking...I mean it, I'm just thinking about it right now..."

"Out with it, woman, what are you thinking about."

"If I decided to move here with Damon, I could still oversee most of the things happening there and maybe expand, add another location, something like that. To do that, I'd need someone to step into my shoes as the manager there. Is that something you would be up for? You don't have to answer me right now. Give it some time and think about it. You can even let me know when you come back from maternity leave."

"I fully support this idea. There's nothing to think about. I'm in."

"You're the best, you know that?"

"Duh. That's why you hired me."

"I guess I should let you go so you can get some work done, eh?" *and so that I can cry like a loon again,* I think to myself.

"If you insist. I'm sure I'll talk to you tomorrow."

"Please keep all of this between you and me for now."

"I got you. I'm not telling anyone. Bye, Maeve!"

Victoria hangs up first, and I focus on emails and verifying this coming week's payroll until a knock on the front door pulls my attention away. I'm unsure if I should answer it or not, especially since Damon said that there shouldn't be any visitors today. Checking out the window, I see a petite girl dressed in overalls with what looks like food in her hands.

It is almost lunchtime. Maybe Damon ordered food to be delivered.

I fumble around in my bag for my wallet and pull out some cash before opening the door.

"Hi there, how much do I owe ya?"

The woman looks at me with a smile, then walks right on past me and into the kitchen.

"Let me set this stuff down here. Shew," the stranger brushes her hands off on the bottom of her overalls before hugging me. "It is so nice to finally meet you, Maeve."

"Uhm. Yeah. Nice to meet you too..." I pause, hoping that she'll tell me her name.

She slaps her forehead, "Oh my Gosh, I've forgotten my manners. I'm Gavin's wife, Quinn."

"Holy shit! You're Quinn! Damon showed me pictures from your wedding! I'm so sorry that I didn't recognize you at first."

"It's okay. Gavin and Damon have been friends for so long that I just make myself at home around here. I wasn't even thinking. I promise to wait until I'm invited in next time."

The backdoor opens, and the two men in question come shuffling in.

"You made it," Gavin pulls his wife in for a hug and a kiss that I'm sure is not meant for anyone else to see.

Damon walks over to me. "I don't smell like shit, yet. Just sweat." He says with a wink as he leans in to give me a peck on the cheek.

"Hey, she didn't gag this time! We're growing on her." Gavin takes the chance to poke fun at me.

"Fuck off," the words are out of my mouth before Damon even has a chance to say them this time.

"She really is catching on, man," Gavin says with a plate already in his hand and helping himself to whatever his wife has brought over. "We should go have lunch on the back of the truck and let these two love birds have some alone time."

"You can eat lunch right here at the table since you're the one who coordinated this whole thing. Last time you two had lunch together, Rawlings caught you humping like rabbits in the hayloft." Damon says while passing me a plate.

"You mean to tell me the poor girl didn't know I was coming? And here I walked in like I owned the place." Quinn scoffs.

"What else is new? You've been walking in like you lived here since we were kids." Damon shrugs.

"She knocked," I add.

Damon's eyes widen in amusement, "Whoa. You know how to knock?"

"I didn't want to scare the girl half to death. Or walk in on something I shouldn't have."

"Like how Maeve walked in on breakfast yesterday in one of Damon's t-shirts." Gavin is dumb enough to add.

Damon quickly sets his plate down and wrestles Gavin into a headlock. "We agreed not to ever speak of that again. Apologize."

I'm not sure if I should try and stop the two of them or let them have at it. Quinn doesn't seem to be phased by it, so I take my cue from her and watch as Gavin decides to fight back.

"If she's going to be hanging around here, she's gotta learn to handle a joke, man." He defends.

"If she's going to be hanging around here or not, you're going to respect her like you would your own wife." Damon grunts as Gavin elbows him in the gut.

"Outside!" I yell. "Both of you. Out!"

Damon doesn't let go. The two manage to scuffle their way out the door. Quinn looks over at me and gives me a high-five.

"They do this at least once a week if someone isn't babysitting them." She tells me.

"Should I be worried?"

"Nah. They'll roll around in the dirt for a few minutes, then come back inside and act like nothing ever happened. Gavin enjoys plucking Damon's nerves. Having you around is one more thing he can torment him with. Don't be afraid to tell Gavin to quit either. He'll listen."

"I didn't mean to walk in on them like that yesterday."

"Hm?" She mumbles over the bite of food she just put in her mouth.

"Walking in on all the guys, in nothing but Damon's shirt. It wasn't on purpose."

"Psh. I heard the whole story. Damon forgot to tell you they would all be here. Maeve, I'm not one you have to worry about. Please don't be intimidated by me."

"You know what's really stupid?"

"What's that?"

"I'm not usually intimidated by anyone. Being here seems to have thrown me through a loop."

"I get it. I moved away for a few years for college. Wanted to see the world and all that. What a wake-up call, ya know? People around here knew me as this girl who could take care of herself. I hung out with everyone, was the life of the party. Wrangled all the boys and kept them in line. Everyone in college thought I was a stuck-up bitch with an attitude problem," she wipes her mouth with a napkin then quickly adds, "not that I'm calling you a stuck-up bitch. I don't think that at all. I barely know you."

"I didn't take it that way."

"What I mean is, when you're someplace new and no one knows you, a place that's so different from what you're used to, it's easy to be thrown off balance."

"You're right. Thanks for saying that."

The boys walk back in, covered in dirt and laughing like a bunch of loons.

Quinn nods her head and says, "Told ya so. Now, eat up before they take it all."

Damon and Gavin eat their lunch then excuse themselves to get back to work, leaving me with Quinn, who ends up spending the afternoon with me. By the time the sun starts to set, I feel like I've known her my whole life.

"Damn, I've been up your ass all day," she chuckles. "Those boneheads should be coming in soon. If y'all don't have plans tonight, you should come down to *Rusty's* with us. He's got some halfway decent food and Monday nights are half-priced beers."

"I'm not really sure what Damon has planned. I'm trying to go with the flow a little more today."

"Well, I'm going to get on down to my house. Ain't no sense in waiting on Gavin. He's got his own truck to drive home. Let me give you my number. You can text me to let me know if y'all are coming. You can text me anytime, really. I could use another girlie friend."

I program Quinn's number in my phone and wait for her to leave before cleaning up the kitchen table where my laptop sits untouched since this morning. By the time I'm done that, Damon is rolling in the door.

"Honey, I'm home," he sing-songs like Ricky from *I Love Lucy*. "and I'm sure I smell much worse now."

I scrunch up my nose. "Eww."

"Shower, then we can figure out dinner. I'll be right back," he blows me a kiss and hustles down the hallway.

TWENTY-SEVEN
DAMON

We manage to make it through our first holiday season together. The time between Thanksgiving and Christmas flies by, with Maeve spending a lot of time in DC working events on her schedule and getting ready for her assistant to go out on maternity leave. Juggling prepping for winter on the farm and making sure I get to see my girl has left little time for sleep on my end.

The time apart is killing me now more than ever. Video calls and text messages aren't cutting it anymore. Not to mention that the time Maeve spends driving back and forth makes me a nervous wreck. Whoever thought this would be easy was crazy. Loving her is damn sure worth it, though.

"How's Marley?" Maeve asks on the other end of the phone. I finished work for today, and now I'm on nurse duty for a mare, Marley, who could give birth in the next day or so.

"She's showing more signs that she's ready. Why do *you* sound like you're driving?"

"Oh, uhm. I needed to pick some things up from the store for dinner."

"Please be safe. Is it snowing there yet?"

"Not yet."

"I still don't like the idea of you going to this event on Saturday in the snow."

I can hear her huff on the other end. "Damon, I'm not going to break. The baby is fine. I'm fine. And a little snow isn't going to hurt anyone. Listen, I just turned into the parking lot. I'll call you later, okay?"

"I love you."

"I love you too, Cowboy."

Gavin comes into the barn as I hang up the phone and kicks my boot, "Hey, lover boy."

"Really, asshole?"

"Wife is going out with some girlfriends tonight. Figured I would keep you company for a while."

I chuckle at Gavin's dumbass. "Keep me company? Aren't you the one scheduled to help if this foal makes her debut tonight?"

"I was trying to make myself sound like the good guy," he hands me a thermos full of coffee. "Last time we spent the night in the barn, we had a bunch of sick horses."

"Don't remind me. I'm hoping tonight won't be so dramatic."

"Hard to believe that was only a few short months ago."

I can tell by his voice that he's fishing for something. "What's your point, Gavin?"

He stuffs his hands in his pockets and whistles. "Just wondering when you're going to pop the question."

"When she's ready."

"Valentine's Day is a few weeks away," Gavin offers up.

"Only the most cliché time to pop the question."

"I happen to have it on good authority that Maeve's

been thinking about wedding plans." His little revelation shocks me.

"The fuck you do." I sputter.

Gavin holds up one hand. "Swear. Last time Quinn had lunch with her. Maeve said that she thinks she's ready for forever."

I try to brush it off. Not because I don't want to marry her. But because I don't need Gavin to run to Quinn and cluck like a chicken, ruining any chance at surprising Maeve. I'll ask her when the time is right for both of us.

About two hours later, the snow has started falling on the ground, and Marley starts transitioning.

We keep our distance but watch over the momma as she starts pushing. Normal deliveries take minutes from the time the foal's hooves are pushed out, but Marley seems to be struggling this time. The delicate dance between letting her birth naturally and saving momma and baby begins.

Gavin calls Keaton to let him know things are happening, then paces like a nervous father, watching the clock. Nearly thirty minutes later, Marley hasn't progressed.

"We need to help her out." He calls it before I have to.

Calmly talking to Marley, I take quick yet cautious steps toward her so that she doesn't spook or stress out more. She grunts as if she understands while I lean down and grab ahold of the legs above the ankles. "Next push, Momma, give it all you got. We're going to help you."

I brace myself with Gavin behind me for extra resistance. Together we both tug with each contraction. Once the head is out, I have to cut open the sac that is still intact so the little one can breathe. Three more hard pulls from us with three exhausted pushes from Marley, the foal is out. Momma lifts her head to look at her baby and gives us a huff.

"Huh, oh my gosh."

Looking over my shoulder, I'm surprised to see Maeve standing outside the stall.

"That's the most breathtaking thing I've ever seen," she sobs.

Gavin gives me a shove. "Go on. They're fine. Keaton will be here soon to check on them. Let's let Marley rest."

"Maeve. What are you doing here?" I reach out to wrap her in my arms, but she takes two steps back and points to the gunk all over me. I chuckle, "Right. I need to clean up. I thought you had to work tomorrow."

"I may have told a white lie. I wanted to surprise you. Looks like Marley had perfect timing."

"Welcome to life on a farm," I tell her while pulling my sweatshirt off and wiping away what I can.

She dabs her eyes, "I can't think of anything more perfect to symbolize a new beginning for us."

"New beginnings?"

"I'm finally *home*."

That stops me in my tracks. "Home."

"Autumn is filling in until Victoria is back. Dad helped me pack up everything I need in a trailer, and I decided that keeping my apartment in DC wasn't so important anymore."

"You've gone and done it now. He's going to hug you, horse gunk and all. No way to escape it," Gavin chuckles.

I have the decency toss my t-shirt for good measure, too, before she's in my arms. "I've waited a long time for this moment."

Maeve squeals and tries to wiggle free. "Ugh. Damon!"

"Might as well get used to it. By this time next year, we'll have you out here with us." I tell her with a kiss.

Gavin quickly chimes in, "She needs muck stalls first!"

"Right. You won't let me muck stalls. I doubt you're going to let me tug a pony out of its momma."

"I'll let you do anything you want, as long as you promise to stay." Blame it on the high from bringing a new life into the world or just knowing that I'll get to fall asleep next to Maeve for the rest of my life. My voice cracks and I fight back the tears of my own.

"Damon," Maeve hisses. "Really. Let me go." I turn her loose, and she gasps for air while coving her mouth. "I think I'm going to be sick."

"We're going to have to work on your queasy stomach."

Maeve rushes to the nearest empty bucket, and we both flip Gavin the middle finger.

Forget waiting for Valentine's Day. Tomorrow is a good a day as any to ask her to be my wife.

EPILOGUE
DAMON

Six and a half months later...

After twelve long hours of labor, Maeve ended up needing a c-section to bring our baby into the world. Still dressed in scrubs from head to toe, I walk out to let our family know the good news now that Maeve and baby are both settled in the post-partum room.

Mom and Dad are huddled together in excitement, and everyone stands when I walk into the room. Looking around at all the people here to celebrate our first child's birth, I'm overwhelmed with love and joy. Aunt Tillie flips her phone around to show – Admiral Peterson's face as soon as she notices me.

"How's my girl?" he immediately asks. Six weeks ago, that promotion finally came through for my soon-to-be father-in-law, along with new orders. I have no idea what time it is where he's at, but I know he's been on the phone as much as he can while we all waited.

"She's doing good. Mom and baby are both great, actually." I tell everyone.

"Well, don't keep us waiting. Is it a boy or a girl?" Of course, it's Gavin who can't keep his mouth shut.

"It's a girl," I know I'm beaming proudly. "Ciara Nova is nine pounds, two ounces, and twenty-one inches. She looks just like her momma."

Cheers erupt around the room, and everyone rushes to congratulation me with hugs and warm wishes.

"Aunt Tillie, our girl, is asking for you. And she wanted me to tell you to keep the Admiral on the line," I tell her with a wink when she finally gets to me. Aunt Tillie steps into the hallway while I let everyone else know that they can come back two at a time after my Mom and Dad.

I meet Aunt Tillie in the hallway and am about to walk her to Maeve's room when I spot Curtis and Stone in the corridor.

"Hey, you two," I clap Curtis on the back and shake Stone's hand. "Mom must have invited the whole town. I appreciate you coming, Stone," I was so caught up in my own world for a moment that I almost missed that they both look like deer caught in headlights. "Whoa. Are you two okay?"

Curtis squeezes the back of his neck and winces. "Actually. Can we...uh... talk for a second?"

"Yeah, man. One second," I turn to Aunt Tillie. "You can go on, so we don't keep Pops tied up. Pass the nurses' station and make a left. Room 222 on the right."

Aunt Tillie nods and leaves me with the guys.

"What's up? Is something wrong?" My own excitement is quickly turning in to worry.

"Yeah. Everything is good. Better than good, actually." He blows out a breath and looks at Stone for confirmation. "You're okay with this, right?"

The other man leans back against the wall with his arms

crossed and his mouth in a tight thin line. One nod is his only response.

"Day, this isn't exactly the time or place I wanted to have this discussion. It's your big day and all. But there's something you should know. About me and Stone, actually."

I HOPE you enjoyed Damon and Maeve's story!

IF YOU'RE SO INCLINED, I would love it if you considered leaving a review. Reviews help authors get seen. It doesn't have to be lengthy or fancy. A line or two will do.

THERE'S plenty more from the Knightly twins in Curtis's story which can be found here:
https://authoraubreevalentine.org/books/knight/

IF YOU'RE interested in bonus scenes, sales and new release updates plus plenty of exclusives – feel free to sign up for my https://authoraubreevalentine.org/newsletter/!

KNIGHT

DAY & KNIGHT SERIES BOOK 2

Curtis Knightly's story happens in Knight – Book 2 of the Day and Knight Series!

Curtis Knightly hated two things...lies and keeping secrets. For the past sixteen years he was guilty of both.

When the pressure of his daily life starts mounting around him, Curtis decides it's time to head back home to rural Pennsylvania for a while.

Trading his fancy suits and high tech computer for cattle and hay bales feels like just what the doctor ordered...that is until his past makes a reappearance and forces him to take a hard look at the choices he's made.

When his vacation is over and it's time to return to the city, Curtis will have to do whatever it takes to prove that second chances are worthy of happy endings, even if that means admitting his own truths to the world.

Keep reading for a sneak peek from Knight

CHAPTER 1

CURTIS

I've been living a lie. For almost twenty years, I've lied to myself and everyone around me. The easiest way to keep up appearances was for me to avoid my hometown and the person who responsible for making me question everything I thought I knew about myself. I haven't set food in Bitterhill since the day I left for the Army.

Leave it to my childhood friend, Gavin, to draw me back home for his wedding.

With my gorgeous fiancée, Gidget, or Gigi for short; on my arm – I'm being forced to face a past that part of me is still desperate for.

Standing up here at the front of the church with my twin brother and Stone Montgomery while Gavin exchanges vows with his lifelong sweetheart, Quinn, is supposed to be an honor. It feels more like a death sentence. This tie feels like a noose around my neck, strangling the life out of me. Sweat is beading around my forehead and if these two don't hurry up and kiss, I might just pass out.

I need a drink. A stiff one. And to get away from everyone else.

Gigi gives me a reassuring smile from the front pew where she's sitting next to my parents. Seeing Mom and Dad again in person only increases the years of guilt I've tried to bury.

Missed holidays. Limited visits to Mom and Dad's place in Florida. I blamed all of it on work. The Army needed me. I couldn't get away. Oops, new orders – sorry, I won't make it.

Instead I left everything up to Damon. He could handle it all. Take over the farm. Check in on Mom and Dad. All while I played G.I. Joe and did everything I could to fight the feelings I struggled with since I was a teen.

Pastor Harold finally pronounces the happy couple as man and wife and Gavin kisses his bride. At least now I can put some space between myself the 285 pounds of muscle standing next to me.

Damon moves first, meeting the maid of honor at the center of the alter and taking her hand. I follow behind him and lace arms with Quinn's younger cousin Ruby to escort her down the aisle to the back of the church.

Gigi works her way through the crowd of guests to find. I put my arm around her and pull her in for a hug with the fake smile that I've mastered over the years.

From the outside looking in, I doubt anyone notices. Except Damon who keeps giving me *the look,* that look that tells me his twin ESP is tingling.

Oh well, he can stop trying to read my mind. There's no way I'm going to open up to him about this. I need to figure this out for myself first.

After all the guests have made it out of the church, the photographer subjects us to even more torture with staged photographs. I'm tired of smiling, and tired of being so close to all these people that I've been hiding from.

"Great, great. One more and then the bridal party is free to go," the photographer poses us together again and snaps away. "Perfect. Bride and Groom, you stay. Everyone else, I'll see you at the reception."

Gigi takes my hand, and we walk out of the church to climb into Damon's truck to head back to the farm.

The moment he parks, I hop out, making a beeline for the bar. There's a whole bottle of whiskey calling my name.

I've got the first glass down by the time Damon finds me.

"Something wrong? You jumped out of my truck like your ass was on fire."

I throw back the second glass, embracing the burn from the dark liquid. If he thinks I'm going to answer that, he's bumped his head.

"Listen, I'm not one to tell you what to do. That said, you might wanna take it easy before you make an ass of yourself. It is Gavin's wedding."

"Just taking the edge off." And it's been a long time since I've gotten drunk enough to make a scene. I know how to hold my liquor.

"Your next glass should probably be water."

Sigh. I hate the fact that Damon has a point. "You're right. Getting drunk isn't going to help matters anyway."

"You keep talking in riddles that make no damn sense."

"Ah, little brother, some things you just wouldn't understand." Maybe if I say it enough, he'll back off.

"Yeah and there you go again. Weirdo. Before you go back to DC, I'm going to get to the bottom of whatever has crawled up your ass."

He's welcome to try. I've mastered the art of keeping secrets. The world is better off that way.

"Whatever. Looks like the newlyweds are here." I nod in their direction. At least those two are happy and in love.

"Saved by the wedding bells...this time."

I roll my eyes and smirk. Saved by the wedding bells, indeed.

FIND Knight – here: https://authoraubreevalentine.org/books/knight/

ACKNOWLEDGMENTS

First and foremost, none of this would ever be possible without the support from my family. Their patience and encouragement sees me through on days when it's hard to even find the time to write.

To Shelley Lange Photography for capturing the image that inspired this entire book, THANK YOU!

Kris Zizzo – I personally could not have asked for a better muse and I feel blessed to call you a friend. Wishing you all the success in the world! Thank you for your support!

Josie – Josie, Josie, Josie...what would I do without you? From (very) late night (or really early morning) conversations when we're both procrastinating, to uhm... "inspiration" and "research" assistance...you keep me sane and entertained.

Lauren – This year brought forth a lot of changes and we've grown so much. I'm incredibly thankful for your never-ending friendship. Thank you for always being up for the challenge when it comes to Alpha or beta reading for my incredibly scattered self. And for always encouraging this punster to PLOT first. I still cannot confirm on deny if plotting works for me...hahaha. You tried. LOL.

Yvette – Your hawk like talent for proofreading is extraordinary. Thank you for all your hard work. It's always an honor to work with you.

Mignon – One of my absolute best friends and a kickass cover designer. I'm forever thankful for your ability to sometimes literally read my mind and bring to life exactly what I'm thinking of, even when I can't quite explain it. Thank you for the countless hours of support, listening and encouragement. Here's to an amazing 2021 for us both!

My readers – Whether you're new or have been with me since the very beginning, if you're reading this right now, THANK YOU. You are a vital roll in my success. I wouldn't be able to chase this dream without you.

Bloggers – I say this every time. You are the live life to this community. Your support is a pivotal key to an author's success. Thank you for your tireless hours promoting, reading and reviewing!

Chances are, I've probably forgotten someone and for that I'm sorry. Know that I love you all and I am forever thankful that I get to chase my dreams with you all.

Xoxo,

Aubree

ABOUT THE AUTHOR

Aubree Valentine began her book world career back in 2016 as a virtual assistant for a friend/author and as a book blogger. While working with authors, PR companies and fellow bloggers, she fell even more in love with the Indie community and decided to launch her own small scale PR company where she continued to hone her skills as a virtual assistant to several authors and studied the ins and outs of what it takes to help succeed in the industry.

In early 2019, during an intense strategy session with one of her favorite author friends, they decided to join forces and take over the world. Or at least combine their know-how and strengths when it comes to all things publishing, for the greater good, and therefore launched Forever Write PR, LLC.

Aubree doesn't always hang out behind the scenes though and has put her business knowledge to good use for herself as well. Her first book, Take Back My Heart, released in the fall of 2016, with its follow up - Come Back to Me launching a year later.

When she's not working with her partner in crime, you

can find her penning fun and flirty stories about all of her imaginary and very smexy alphas. This includes her current and most popular series, Too Hot To Handle.

Aubree has a degree in sarcasm and resides in Pennsylvania. She enjoys reading, chasing after her twins and her three furbabies, cuddling with her husband, and coming up with new project ideas that often involve power tools.

She's usually always online via Facebook or Instagram @authoraubreevalentine.

www.aubreevalentine.org

STAY CONNECTED

Come join my reader group on Facebook!
https://www.facebook.com/groups/AubreeVReaderGroup/
Stay up-to-date on new releases, information, and exclusive content. Sign up for my newsletter!
https://authoraubreevalentine.org/newsletter/
Find me on social media:
Facebook
Twitter
Instagram
BookBub
Goodreads
Pinterest

ALSO BY AUBREE VALENTINE

Too Hot to Handle Series

Hot Cop

Cop Tease

Strip Search

Cop Blocked

Covert Affair – Coming Soon

Wild Fire – Coming Soon

Fed Up – Coming Soon

425 Madison Series

Love Under Construction

Love Under Protection

Susan Stoker's Badge of Honor World

Justice for Danielle

Come Back To Me Series

(Currently unavailable)

Take Back My Heart

Come Back To Me

Anthologies

(The following are no longer available:)

Victory is Sweet

Paperback Writers

Rocked to The Core

Playing to Win

Snowed Inn

Made in the USA
Monee, IL
18 January 2021